B E S T
B L A C K
WOMEN'S
EROTICA 2

B E S T
B L A C K
WOMEN'S
EROTICA 2

Edited by

Samiya A. Bashir

CLEIS PRESS

Published in the United States by Cleis Press Inc.,
P.O. Box 14684, San Francisco, California 94114.
Printed in the United States.
Cover design: Scott Idleman
Text design: Frank Wiedemann
Logo art: Juana Alicia
First Edition.
10 9 8 7 6 5 4 3 2 1

*For my grandmothers, my mothers, my sisters, and my aunts.
For all the women whose love of life and zest
for loving fully and completely informs me.
For the freaky black girls everywhere who continue
to liberate our bodies and our minds.*

*Love is lak de sea. It's uh movin' thang, but still and all,
it takes its shape from de shore it meets, and it's different with
every shore.*
　　　—Zora Neale Hurston, *Their Eyes Were Watching* God

*Please get over the notion that your particular "thing" is
something that only the deepest, saddest, the most nobly tortured can know. It ain't. It's just one kind of sex—that's all.
And in my opinion, the universe turns regardless.*
　　　　　　　—Lorraine Hansberry

TABLE OF CONTENTS

Introduction
Samiya A. Bashir

Touch. Like the pages of this volume, we all need to be
touched, caressed, flipped, turned, and read with passion. Our
senses need inspiration to open and flare, to allow the flow
of sensory input, ever present in our world, to wash through
our bodies and into the spiritual realm housed within. All too
often we go through our everyday lives, accepting an increas-
ing amount of input and information, rarely even stopping to
filter it, or (rarer still) insisting on that input which strokes
and kisses our imaginations.

I hope that this collection does just that. I hope these stories
stretch their tender fingertips to touch you, the reader, in ways
that force you to stop and enjoy the sensation. In compiling
and constructing this second edition of *Best Black Women's
Erotica,* it was important both to be true to the scope of
the series and to offer something unique in the process. As I
accepted this challenge I reached back to mine my own trunk
of memories. I wanted to find not only moments of change and
growth, but the inspiration for those moments. What I found
illuminated the idea of difference. In this collection, it was

important for me to present as wide a berth of black women's experience as possible. The range—which covers age, region, physical ability, sexual orientation, identity, and the multiple types of relationships we create for ourselves—hopes to provide a mirror for some women, and a window to others.

Best Black Women's Erotica 2 includes twenty stories written by women from diverse backgrounds, each with a unique story to tell. The volume opens with "Rhythm," Donna Sherard's examination of the erotic in everyday experience. The story takes one woman, getting her hair braided by two experts while waiting for the return of her lover, into the dreamworld of fantasy, led by touch.

Opal Palmer Adisa and D. H. Brent craft characters for whom the relationship is not the point, or so they hope; the point is the need to be fulfilled, to feel as the light inside the spark. Camille Banks-Lee, folade mondisa speaks-love, and Michele Elliott imagine relationships that celebrate their sexual selves. Love is explored through the telephone wires and Internet cables, inspired by music and film, and takes place in spaces at once familiar, changed, and completely new. "Palimpsest," by R. Erica Doyle, takes readers' expectations, and any last grasp at taboo, and puts them through the spin cycle, tumbling faster and faster until they jerk to a stop, and come out hot, changed, slightly singed, and with the smell of rebirth.

The things that we choose to eroticize also speak volumes about how we filter all that input. Robin G. White's story of a gospel organist and her congregant, "Shout," draws a direct line between the physical and the spiritual, inviting readers to "feel the spirit" in a whole new way. Tracy Price-Thompson mines a driving need that pushes far past fleeting lust to find strength in the desolation of a desert war. In "Shared Heat," she brings together a photographer and an infantry commander leading his troops to a hopeless and probably pointless death. Their near-wordless exchange must pack the explosive passion of a lifetime into one cold, silent night. Kimberly White looks into a future where the line between the breath of life and the blink of automation merges with a woman and her made-to-order lover.

Throughout this collection, the senses are engaged. In Kiini Ibura Salaam's "Kai Does Red...Again" the story is told to the backbeat of the club music threatening to burst through the bathroom door. Tara Betts explores the sense of sound and the sensuality of speech in "Talk to Me." Janeé Bolden uses hip-hop as a metronome, and Dorothy Randall Gray's full, powerful, and sensual "Miss Cicero" finds her passion reading Zora Neale Hurston to a longtime friend. In the end, Carol Smith Passariello uses the photographer's lens to break through the barriers of fear and shame as a group of friends learn together how to find their own inner and outer beauty.

Take it in all at once, or stretch it with slow, savory sips. Let the stories enfold you for a moment, let them touch and stroke you, body and spirit. Drink them in, spit them back out if you like, but savor the taste. These stories will have you coming back for more.

Samiya A. Bashir
New York
December 2002

Samiya A. Bashir

Rhythm
Donna Sherard

Living in Kampala requires patience to learn to flourish within the rise and fall of natural movements that mark the passage of the day. Watches are rendered unnecessary. Each day falls into a calculated and undulating rhythm. To the newly initiated, this rhythm creates what may seem to be a haphazard and unplanned environment, regularly punctuated by daily electricity outages, quizzical traffic patterns, and phone delays. I have just begun to realize, however, that only a fool would try to define or label this city as anything abnormal or disorganized. I have begun to understand that life in Kampala, and especially during the rainy season, is managed by a seductive rhythm guided by daylight and rain that is very methodical, indeed. I have also had to come to terms with the reality that living here happily requires adjustment to this rhythm. Everything here moves to the calculated staccato, yielding a magic that can only be described as both expected and yet very unexpected.

Every day, Kampala's rhythm starts at just before sunrise when something in the easy breeze encourages the rooster, owned by the neighboring guesthouse, to croak his morning alarm. After three weeks of mornings here with Daudi, I have come to understand the wakeup pattern of our cackling neighbor. His voice is comically rusty at first, sounding almost like a human imitation. Soon after his warm-up, however, his lubricated and lusty vocal cords break out into full alto vibrato that sounds from within the confines of his breast, and screams through his beak.

This Friday, this day fourteen of my twenty-eight-day cycle, also began with the familiar moist pressure in my loins that accompanied the rooster's orchestrated cries. Thirty was seemingly now a curse, as sex for me had lost some of its wild abandon. My innate, physical desire "to get some" was usually now at its greatest crescendo only when I was also feeling the pinch of ovulation. This morning, and in its own timely rhythm, nature's desire to reproduce woke me with an insuppressible and very hopeful horniness. The hopefulness was, unfortunately, irrelevant, for this morning was different. Daudi wasn't here. Having traveled home to Nairobi for work almost a week ago, he wouldn't be coming back until well after Kampala's day's end, long after sundown, and long after the pungent smell of smoking rot—Friday's burned garbage—had blown to the bottom of the hill.

Today was also the first day of the rainy season, and while it had not yet rained, its promise left our bedroom humid. The still uncooled mid-April heat made the mosquito net feel thick as cheesecloth. I lay still as my overactive imagination felt Daudi's fingers moving up my legs and, finding the joining of my thighs soaking wet and my clitoris hard as tanzanite, he would then straddle me and we'd make love. I was left to merely imagine, however, to bookmark that thought for this evening. Lying spread-eagled across our bed reminded me, again, that he was still not here.

Before he left on Monday we had lain on this same bed

together, still sweaty and nude from our preliminary good-byes. I watched his profile as his lips spilled a litany of concerns about leaving me alone, in his deep Kikuyu accent. This one week would be our longest separation since I had returned, and he sounded frighteningly like my father.

"Remember to call Wamala if you need to go anywhere, and please don't forget to lock the car doors at the roundabouts. Can you remember to close the windows at night and spray the room and turn on the mosquito zappers?"

Daudi was forever worried about my falling victim to crimes usually reserved for Muzungus and other foreigners in traffic, and he took my Michigan blood—and the fact that it had not yet been baptized with malaria—as his single greatest responsibility.

"Babes, I will be fine," I had assured him.

In actuality, while not at all terrified at his leaving me alone in this house shortly after my relocation here, I had struggled with the onset of two emotions: first, hating that we were about to be separated even for a week so soon after our previous nine-month hiatus, and second, hating the fact that I was feeling so damn needy.

Last Monday, the prospect of the one-week separation had seemed like a lifetime, and I was now emotionally and very physically anxious for his return. Daudi and I, both far too cynical to have pet names for our body parts, never baptized his penis or my vagina with any names other than "dick" and "pussy" (words whose meanings had thankfully transcended our cross-cultural backgrounds). Today, I could think of nothing but their reacquaintance as I opened my eyes on this Friday. With the persistent throbbing in my crotch bordering on ridiculous, I allowed a fleeting thought of quenching my own thirst through a brief tangle with my makeshift soapstone dildo—originally, a mildly phallic-shaped figurine Daudi had brought me from Nairobi. I quickly changed my mind as I remembered that for the past three nights, this had already proved to be an unsatisfying option. While certainly hard, the figurine never seemed to get warm enough, and certainly didn't vibrate like "Pinky," whom I had left in the States for fear of embarrassment at the Ugandan customs inspection. Although I smiled to myself at the thought of the soaking-wet welcome Daudi would come home to tonight, I somehow knew that my decision to not masturbate away my inflated libido this morning would have its own frustrating consequences.

The sun, now close to full throttle, decorated the bedroom with stripes as it passed through the glass-levered windows. The rooster's cacophony had now yielded to the next round of sounds that marked the slow unfolding of the morning. They began in perfectly timed succession with the barking of the German shepherds that volunteered to guard the neighboring Kabira School. The dogs knew, by the tilt of the sun, when breakfast would be tossed at them through the kitchen doors. At the same time, our version of a motorized rush hour passed with the buzzing sound of the moped *boda-boda* taxis that ferried neighbors to the more well traveled Kironde Road. I knew that as they became less frequent it was getting past any acceptable time to get up. My punishment would certainly be meted out if I still found myself lying here unwashed and unfed to hear the slight click of the daily, induced off-cycle of our electricity, and the whirring swell of the generator next door, indicating the end of hot water and the ability to cook my breakfast, not having a generator ourselves. Again, slow to adjust to Kampala's own means of telling time, I still had to confirm through a roll of my body toward the bedroom digital clock what this city already knew, that it was eight A.M., just one hour before my nine o'clock appointment with the hair braiders.

After getting dressed, I moved downstairs to sit close enough to the door to listen for what would undoubtedly be a very soft knock. Ugandan women, as was culturally prescribed, usually tapped to announce their presence in the same hushed tones in which they spoke. Their voices often so quiet, they encouraged a natural intimacy, as I was often forced to lean into their breath to have any conversation at all.

As I waited, I sat watching little colored birds dancing though the bush outside our window like confetti, basking in what would undoubtedly be one of their last dry mornings for a while. Having lived through last year's rainy season, I knew today would probably see the sun alternate with the clouds until the clouds, swollen and dark, finally relieved themselves of very heavy rain that would last for weeks.

I then heard it, the soft "brush-tap" on the door followed by muffled female voices.

I opened the door and Penninah stood under the now darkened but still dry sky, with one other woman. The woman, while striking, bore the telltale orange-tinged face and dark walnut neck that betrayed her use of Fair and Light bleaching cream. Upon my beckoning, they waved into the foyer with a quick gust that simultaneously rustled their skirts and the black plastic cavera undoubtedly holding my new hair.

"Good morning, Madame," they both said with smiles.

"Good morning, please come in."

They entered and their sandals shuffled on the tile floor. As they moved past me I felt a tingling, surprisingly erotic warmth that transformed my entryway and enveloped the energy Daudi and I had created in this house together.

"Madame," Penninah hush-whispered. "Where shall we work?"

"Penninah, please call me Nicole, and we can do the braiding in the living room," I said. While Ugandans held tightly to the formal systems of social order that designated me as "Madame," at merely age thirty, I was having a problem with conforming.

Penninah smiled, acknowledging my request, and turned to introduce her partner. "Nicole, this is Biira."

Biira, quickly looking at me and then away, shook my hand in hers. While she gripped my extended hand very lightly I felt a warmth travel the length of my forearm. As we stood I felt them both quietly assessing my short Afro, undoubtedly calculating how it would braid, and how long we would be there together.

We moved to the next room where I had already pulled our most comfortable, cushioned wicker chair to the middle of the floor. The room was now sun-filled and the curtains, billowing with the breeze, seemed to welcome the women into its confines.

"You'll sit there?" Penninah half asked, half stated.

"Yes, will that be OK?" I asked, not sure if they would find the height appropriate.

"It is fine." She turned to say something in Luganda to Biira and it was then that I realized that Biira was not shy as much as just not comfortable with English, and somewhat still in shock as she discovered through my accent that I was something she had never seen: an American who was also black. Penninah and I had met before; I guess she had not passed along what I had long ago discovered to be very big news here in Uganda.

Penninah gestured to the chair and I sat. They both stood over me, gently pulling at my short hair and briefly feeling my roots with their thumbs and forefingers. As they moved closer to either side of me, I could feel the convection of their heat and smell a hint of breakfast on their breath as they spoke.

"Nicole, is this natural or is there something in your hair?" Penninah asked as she stroked the curls behind my ear. In spite of the fact that any arousal caused by her touch was obviously unintentional—she, of course, couldn't know what Daudi's touch behind my ear usually made me do—I felt a warm rush between my legs.

"I have a texturizer," I confessed, hesitantly.

"OK," she said. And with that they swept into fluid action, moving to the dining table to pull from the plastic bag the reddish brown hair they would soon attach to my head.

"We must first divide the hair, and we need Vaseline," Penninah said softly, over her shoulder.

As Penninah spoke, I was lost in the contrast of Biira's skin, orange and then fading to black as her chest disappeared under her clothes. Her white blouse was missing a button, for which she compensated with a safety pin between her breasts. I watched her hips shift underneath her floral skirt as she balanced on one leg then the other, matching the rhythm of her arms separating small pieces of hair from the large, stringy wad that lay on the table.

"I'm sorry, do either of you want some tea, or juice?" Clearly I had forgotten my manners as I bounced back from my stare.

Penninah repeated this in Luganda, to which Biira quietly responded, "Just water, please."

As I poured water into a glass I looked out of the window above the sink at the swaying banana leaves to the left of our driveway. The sky had suddenly turned a foreboding and dark slate blue, playing a deep contrast to the green leaves. I heard an engine stutter on somewhere in the distance and wondered why the presence of these women was causing me chills and why I found my eyes lingering a little too long on Biira. While I could blame sexual neglect from the past week, I still felt somewhat guilty. I felt so close and private here in my home with Daudi. It had become just us, physically and emotionally. We had not had many guests since my return and, instead, spent much of our weekends naked, rediscovering beauty marks and hot-spots. Today, with the arrival of the braiders, however, I felt a hot swelling very familiar and yet very different; our love nest had been temporarily recolored. The thought of sitting between these two women fondling my head as twelve hours passed created an arousing warmth I thought was now reserved only for Daudi, or at the very least for men. As I finished in the kitchen, listening to the low hum of Penninah and Biira's voices, I felt my nipples harden under my T-shirt like two kernels of corn.

With the hair finally separated and me seated in the wicker chair, Penninah and Biira gathered around and above me as if I were a baby in a bassinet. While I had had my hair braided before, I had never sensed this energy. Never had I noticed the harmony of movements that were sensually orchestrated to make me beautiful.

For one minute it was silent in the living room as I watched Biira stroke the first clump of hair with Vaseline until it stiffly matted. After she separated the first small strand and handed it to Penninah, I felt a tiny pinch as Penninah grabbed my first tuft of hair, and their rhythm began.

"The first part of the braiding takes long," Penninah reminded me as she introduced the pattern of their work. "We start with the edges and make sure they are dense."

Of course this I knew, but Penninah wanted to prevent any prematurely impatient squirming of my ass.

With each passing of a greased strand from Biira, Penninah twisted the attachment to the base of my hair in a one-two-three rhythm. I felt Penninah's hands work quickly as she attached and began the twist, leaving the open ends for Biira to finish.

Biira, smelling of blue soap laundry tablets mixed with sweat, was quiet as she moved in time with Penninah, almost as if she were dancing around the perimeter of the chair in the same one-two-three rhythm. Quietly she fought to keep up with Penninah's speed. Each twist was a stroke to my scalp that, though it felt tugged slightly, never hurt.

One-two-three.

On three, the light seemed to dim even further and within minutes a tapping-thud-patter of the first sprinkle of heavy raindrops hitting the patio sounded through the open window. The rainy season often started this way here, with a quick introduction of rain that only forebode the onset of later, much heavier storms.

"Eh-eh, it is the first rain," Biira barely breathed in uncomfortable English. Her words, hitting the back of my neck, raised a shudder.

"Are you cold, Nicole?" Penninah felt my reaction.

"Oh, I'm fine. I guess it's just because the sun went down."

As Penninah's one-two-three came to a complete stop just above my ear, the rain finished. The watchman passed by the window with his late-morning snack of chapatti and tea, and Biira started to finish the second round of twists. She wrapped with a quick motion that made the tips of her fingers sound short tapping noises, which, besides our breathing, was the only sound in the room. I felt the slight rocking vibration of her twists on my scalp as she worked down each shaft of hair.

Biira was short but not small and as she twisted, starting closer to my scalp and working outward, she brushed my shoulder with her soft, low breasts. I felt her even breath and self-consciously thought that perhaps she and Penninah broke the monotone by conversing among themselves with only their eyes, about the condition of my hair or my scalp.

One-two-three.

The women's rhythm dissolved the morning and welcomed the afternoon. The light of the room repeatedly changed as the sun and the clouds continued to trade places. Their work was silent except for their breath, the shuffle of their shoes as they circled to each new position, and the slight tapping noise their fingertips made with each twist of hair. Left with nothing to do, I closed my eyes to the tempo of the one-two-three rhythm

Penninah started and Biira finished, as she twisted each braid to its end.

We sat in my living room alone. I watched in silence, naked Biira dipping her hands in the Vaseline jar and smearing herself, instead of the strands of hair, with the greasy clumps. She made circular patterns on her skin, one-two-three, as she sat shyly stealing glances at me from my couch. I briefly wondered how I would explain the oily stain she was undoubtedly leaving. I watched the movements of her hands rise up to her neck, and she worked her knobby fingers along her fading cream line. She rubbed in the same one-two-three rhythm, rubbing until the line smeared into the oily massage, as if it were only an ink pen mark, and then disappeared. She sat there finally, completely and smoothly deep, dark brown, holding her breasts just under her slightly contrasting nipples. Her nipples, now standing erect above her fingers, were wide and shiny with oil. I moved to sit next to her full body on the couch as she looked at me through her sleepy eyelids, and again I felt her hush-whisper to me in uncomfortable English, mixed with her native Luganda, "Nyabo lean this way...Nyabo...?"

"Nicole?"

Realizing I had dozed, the pull of the one-two-three twisting brought me back to my living room, but this time with my eyes really open.

"Nicole, lean to Biira just a little bit." Penninah's voice broke through. Biira was now behind me, fully dressed, still half-bleached and steadily working on my crown.

"Were you sleeping?" Penninah asked.

I thought that not that much time had passed, but the position of the sun and the cramp of my stomach insisted it was just past lunchtime.

A mild discomfort dampened my hunger. Now fully awake, the one-two-three rhythm on my scalp vibrated my memory. I tried to twist my head up at Biira to see her face. Was she really there with me? I caught a glimpse of her just as her heavy-lidded eyes grazed mine, and without stopping the rhythm of her twisting she coaxed a soft, silent smile from her lips.

I guess that was a fantasy I just slipped into about this woman. A fantasy with thoughts that seemingly violated every code of "man loves woman and woman loves man" in Uganda. I quickly tried to dismiss the little episode, blaming boredom, the warmth of the air, and the lulling intimacy of the braiding for coaxing me to this place. To a place where I thought I wanted, for one minute, to forget about both Daudi and "codes" and feel a different sort of passion.

I shifted my hips to feel whether I was really as wet as I thought.

"Nicole, it is now three. Are you restless? Do you need to get up?" Penninah, an expert braider, was very keen on the temperaments of her clients, and tried to assess the cause of my anxious movement. I rationalized that there was just no way she and Biira were complicit in my delicious mental wanderings. She just couldn't imagine the real reason for the shift of my hips.

"You know, I...I would like to get up for some water and a banana. Can I get you anything?" I asked, as I discovered with a private little rub of my thighs that I really was as wet as I thought.

One-two-three, Biira's fingers tapped a twist to its finish, down my cheek.

Another discussion in Luganda revealed that Biira also wanted a banana and another glass of water. Apparently, Penninah never ate on the job. I got up to move to the kitchen, simultaneously stretching my legs. As I handed the banana and water to Biira I again tried to look her in the eyes to see if she knew what I knew, if she knew about the Vaseline, and the couch. She looked away as she reached for the food and thanked me in Luganda, "Webale nyo."

"Just two more hours, Nicole. We have to finish the last section and then do some trimming. OK? We should be finished by 5:30," Penninah assured me.

I kept my eyes open and watched and listened to Friday pass on and the sun return through the windows. Lulled into a stupor again with the twisting one-two-three, I felt the heavy slide of my eyelids.

Biira was leaving. She stood up from the couch to silently leave and then turned to me as I sat where she had left me on the couch. Her body was magnificent, still lightly gleaming from the Vaseline she lowered to her knees as I sat. As she leaned into my body, her slightly folded stomach resting on my shins, I felt her breathing. Biira slowly worked her knobby hand between my still-shut thighs, traveling up my legs slowly.

One-two-three.

Again, the watchman passed by the window.

I looked down to follow her movements and was startled to discover that I, too, was naked. My full brown curls stood from between my legs, slightly damp from perspiration. Shit!...how would I hide the wet spot I was undoubtedly leaving on the cushion? Shit again!...how was this woman making me so wet? Biira reached up to touch me...sliding her still-oiled palms up the length of my now-parted thighs, and I realized we still had not spoken. I wanted her anyway.... She seemed to read my thoughts. She seemed to know I wanted to feel her mouth on my....

"Hello? Hey, sweetheart."

Biira looked up at me from between my legs with her hooded eyes, but her full lips were still. That accent was not hers; it was not even Ugandan; it was not even a woman's voice at all.

Sweetie?...

I shook awake. "Nicole?"

My head was bowed and as I opened my eyes I saw through my new hanging twists that the same brown loafers I had sent Daudi away with on Monday were somehow on the floor in front of me.

One-two-three, Biira never stopped.

"Babes, you're back," I said sleepily. As I came to I felt strangely embarrassed. It took me a minute to realize I was not naked, and apparently I was the only one who knew about my quick affair. Even Biira twisted on, one-two-three, with hardly a hesitation.

I looked up in time to catch Daudi's shoulders bouncing with his teasing, mock laughter.

"You were out, Bwana."

"Hi, I'm Daudi." He directed his voice above my head to both Biira and Penninah.

"Hello," they both replied softly.

"We are almost done. We just have to trim the hair," Penninah assured him.

"Hey, sweetie," I tried to recover, passing my hands over my lips. "You're early."

As Daudi set his bag down and disappeared for a beer, his voice sailed back to the living room. "I took an earlier flight. Surprise!"

He returned to sit on the couch across from us while they finished trimming, and then he started chattering something about his week. Even the snipping seemed to clip in the same rhythm, one-two-three.

I felt exposed, but my visit with Biira was unfinished. Daudi had unknowingly interrupted something terribly delicious. I clearly wasn't going to be able to get it back with an audience. Especially an audience of my lover.

Unfortunately, too soon the rhythm of Penninah and Biira ended. They seemed to know they were now unwanted. They briskly cleaned the littering hairs from the floor, collected payment, and breezed out of the door in almost the same way they came in. From the doorstep I stood watching them, especially Biira, as the evening breeze lifted her skirt from her hips. Thanks to the now-shining sun, I could see the slight silhouette of her thighs through the fabric. She didn't turn, she just disappeared with Penninah through the black iron gate of our compound, and the watchman closed the latch behind them. Clearly my tangle with Biira, albeit purely mental, was nothing, I rationalized. I was obviously just really horny. As the gate clanged shut, I felt Daudi's familiar hands circle my stomach. "Your hair looks nice."

"Thanks," I said, turning to him.

Our bodies felt humid as we, against all local social taboos, tongue-kissed publicly on our doorstep. I am sure we drew the horrified stares of our missionary neighbors, but I didn't really care.

As I pressed my groin against his, Biira's tapping fingers seemed to disappear. Perhaps her imagined touch was merely an appetizer as I remembered all the familiarity of this man.

While it is hard to run upstairs in flip-flops, while stripping naked, we made it to our bedroom just as the pinkening-dusk sky started to stain our white curtains. As we somehow fell sideways on our mattress, I could smell the toxic beginnings of burning garbage seeping through the screen. We lay there for a minute, Daudi's body cupping my backside, then he slipped his fingers in me, feeling the wet remnants of my adultery. The swell of his dick against my ass assured me he thought it was all about him.

"Did you miss me, Bwana?" he gruffly whispered against the back of my neck, now covered with braids.

I didn't answer, I just rolled backward and lifted my ass so that I could grind my hips on his until he entered me. After some twelve hours of foreplay, making love was out of the question. I needed Daudi to fuck me. Daudi knew my rhythm and asked no questions as he rolled me over with force to enter me from behind. There was absolutely nothing like the way his dick filled every corner of my slick core, the way his balls danced against my ass with each hopeful thrust of his hips.

"Where are you, Bwana?" I eventually asked, as his middle finger so deftly massaged my clitoris. "I'm not gonna last long," I warned.

"I'm at eight," he huffed. We often played a numbers game: putting numerical values on our proximity to orgasm.

Good, I thought. As our scale was one to ten, ten being climax, I would not have to feel that little tingle of guilt that sometimes riddled my gut after belting out an orgasm, and leaving him to pump for himself.

With that encouragement he slid both of his hands to my hanging breasts, gripping them like bicycle handles, and continued to thrust into me. With a twist of my body I gently coaxed him to his back. My swollen pussy needed the attention that only "woman on top" could most often achieve, and I ferociously gripped the wooden headboard as I lowered myself onto his graciously slick and standing dick.

The corners of Daudi's eyelids wrinkled with a slight encouraging smirk as he grabbed my hips and aided my undulation. I shut my eyes just as my upper thighs clenched and I felt the rumbling rise of glorious orgasm fan itself from the base of my spine and rise through my ass. With each slurping dig of my pussy my breath took on sound and I stuttered a moan.

Daudi's hands kneading my ass onto his dick got more vigorous as the final convulsion of orgasm swept me to lower to his chest, allowing our nipples to play a sticky form of tag. As my entire body quivered, he pounded and purred in perfect rhythm, "I've got you, Bwana, I've got you."

I felt his familiar rising moan with my chin at the base of his neck, and he got louder as he came in me in short thrusts of his thick, warm fluid. I relaxed into a full collapse on his chest and measured his racing heart with my sternum while he circled my dripping back with his arms.

As we lay, I nearly felt the commencing first storm of the rainy season as the tapping-thud of heavy raindrops rose to rapid-fire thunder on the balcony outside our door. The rain simultaneously washed away sunset, the stench of the trash, and the conflict of my philandering thoughts. Another tapping rhythm—one-two-three—brought on evening in Kampala, as I listened to the rise of Daudi's soft snore.

Kai Does Red...Again
Kiini Ibura Salaam

Kai felt a hand nudge her in the small of her back. She turned to see Red standing there, grinning like a jack-o'-lantern, a Cheshire cat, or anything with more teeth than mouth. She smiled, then looked away, knowing he would want to know where was that phone call she had promised him when he was deep inside her making her gasp for breath and hold down the sounds that she knew would wake her roommates. Over his shoulder, she could see the bodies humping and jerking on the dance floor. He waited silently as she pushed her hair back and fastened her eyes on his chest. She felt him searching her face for answers as her eyes wandered down his body, stopping finally at his feet.

"Look at those shoes," she said.

"D'ya like them? They're so comfortable," he said, eyes pleading, mouth still cracked in two.

"They're kind of strange," she said and paused. Her gaze left the shoes, ran up his legs, and hovered over the flat brown stomach peeking out beneath his shirt. "But I like your pants."

"My shoes, my pants. Woman, is that all you have to say?"

Kai threw a darting glance into the expectation hovering over his face, then tilted her face up to the ceiling. She shrugged her shoulders and shifted uncomfortably. He continued grinning. She could feel his energy reaching for her, could feel the tension radiating from his body. She leaned back and rested her hip against the bar. A skinny, glossy girl with a lit cigarette and an overflowing cosmopolitan wedged her way between them. Red grabbed Kai by the waist as soon as the girl had slithered past. His hands on her waist were solid and confident, as they had been when he was dragging her across her futon, lifting her knees, spreading her open, guiding her into one position after another. Kai obeyed the pressure of Red's hands and squeezed through the sweaty crowd. Situating herself in a quiet corner near the restroom, she turned to face Red with crossed arms and raised eyebrows.

"Talk to me," Red said.

Kai looked straight into his eyes and said nothing. How do you tell a man his dick is sweet but you don't quite like the rest of him? A smirk slipped over her lips as her mind maniacally worked through phrases and explanations.

"Kai," Red said.

Kai snapped out of her thoughts and focused on Red again. His dark chocolate skin, his glimmering eyes, his wide grin, the disarming energy that overwhelmed her—all threatened to swallow her whole.

"Listen, what happened last week was good, but it was… totally…unexpected, and I thought I'd just let it ride."

The words came slowly, in hesitant spurts, then tumbled out in a quick jumble of words.

"What do you mean, let it ride?" Red asked, gently hooking his finger into the front pocket of Kai's jean skirt.

"I mean," Kai said, letting out a heavy breath, "let it be a one-time thing."

Red drew away from her, his bright eyes momentarily falling dark.

"You mean not do it again?"

Kai shook her head.

"But it was good, Kai, too good. You trying to tell me you wasn't feeling it?"

"I was feeling it, I was. I…."

Kai broke into a smile and stepped away from Red.

"What's up, baby? How you?" she asked, giving a short, dreadlocked man a hug.

"Chillin'," he whispered, placing a kiss full on her mouth. "You're looking scrumptious."

"Thanks, baby."

Kai could feel Red's frustration building behind her. She turned and rested her hand on Red's wrist. Her other hand was linked in the crook of Bey's elbow.

"Red, Bey. Bey, this is Red."

Bey grunted a nondescript greeting in Red's direction. Red crossed his arms and slid a hard glance over Bey's body.

"Alright sis, I see you're busy," Bey said, returning Red's challenge with a brief display of menace.

Kai let a guilty smile slip across her lips.

"I'mma be at the other side of the bar, so come check me when you're done," Bey said, dismissing Red with a flick of his eyes.

"Yeah, a lil later," she murmured and watched Bey saunter away.

"Kai, I don't get you," Red said as soon as Bey was out of earshot.

Kai whipped around to face Red.

"What?"

"You chasing after niggas who won't give you the time

19

of day. That dude was in here ignoring you the night I met you. I'm all up in your ass and you don't want nothing to do with me."

Kai leaned back and put her hands on her hips.

"I don't know you, Red. I spent one night with you. One."

"And how many nights you spent with him?"

Kai let out an irritated sigh.

"What's your point?"

Kai didn't hear Red's point. While he was arguing his case, she felt a hand squeeze her shoulder. She turned and dropped a little exclamation of delight from her lips. Red watched as Kai fell into some man's embrace without even saying, "excuse me." Her head was tilted back as she giggled, laughing flirty words into this new man's ear, behaving as if Red wasn't in the middle of a conversation with her. Behind Kai's back, Red nodded a cold greeting to the stranger. The stranger raised his eyebrow and inclined his head just briefly enough for Red to know that he had seen him. Within seconds Red could hear the man saying good-bye. As soon as the stranger turned away, Red grabbed Kai by the arm and dragged her into the restroom. He slammed the door and locked it.

"So you don't want to fuck with me?" Red asked.

"No," said Kai. "I don't."

Red turned away from Kai and hung his hands on top of his head. Kai leaned against the door and trained her eyes on the dirty vinyl floor.

"Kai, I done slept with a million women, so I know what it's like when it's good. I know when I find somebody who can really ride with me, and you take me there, Kai. The way you were riding me...."

Kai held up her hand for Red to stop. Visions of her sitting on Red's lap, one foot on the restroom trash can, the other hugging the porcelain of the toilet, invaded her mind. Red saw the look on her face and moved in close.

"You were with me, Kai, I can see it on your face. Why are you denying it?"

Kai wouldn't speak. She let her eyes drift up to Red's. His face hovered just inches from hers. In the silence, she felt his hands go to her waist, his mouth go to her throat. She let out a breath of tension.

"Red, just stop."

Red pulled his lips away from Kai's neck.

"Kai, you know you like it."

"I like it, OK. I like it. Does that make you feel better?"

"No, you know what would make me feel better?" Red asked as he ran his hand up the front of Kai's skirt, his fingers nestling in the fold of Kai's thighs before barely brushing between her legs.

Kai pushed Red's hand away from her body.

"Red, I'm not going to lie to you. I enjoyed it. I enjoyed fucking you. I still think about it. Daily. But…."

"But what?"

"But…." Kai paused and looked up into Red's face. "But you're not a package."

Red stepped back and stared at Kai from a distance.

"A package? What are you talking about?"

"Relationship material. 'The one.' I'm trying to be in a relationship. Kicking it ain't gonna get it no more."

Red dismissed Kai's words with a wave of his hand. He leaned his hand on the door next to Kai's ear. She could feel the heat from his wrist radiating on her neck. For a moment everything was still. Kai stared into the shine dancing in Red's eyes, barely breathing as he leaned into her, chest brushing against the tips of her breasts. Then she felt the full weight of him, pressing against her body, pushing her spine against the restroom door. She shifted under his hips and cleared her throat.

"Sex isn't everything, Red," she mumbled, trying to

pretend that her skin wasn't burning, that her heart wasn't pounding, that a throb wasn't building from between her legs to her navel.

"Right now it is," he whispered as he ran his fingers over her bare arm. A tingle sprang up under his touch. The tingle was quickly replaced by sudden sparks of pain as Red bit into her arm. Kai groaned and arched her back, grinding her belly into his waist. He slipped his hands under the back of her shirt and pulled her closer. *C'mon, baby,* his eyes said, *let's fuck now.* Kai leaned her forehead against his chin.

"You have a condom?" she asked.

"Yeah."

Kai looked into Red's face as if searching for the truth. Red grinned eagerly.

"You better not be lying to me. I don't care how hard you get, I ain't fucking you without a condom."

"I got one, I swear."

"Red," Kai said and pushed him away, "why are you doing this?"

"Because your pussy is sweet," Red said and slipped his hand under her skirt, squeezing Kai behind her knee, "and I got to get back up in there."

Kai's eyes flickered closed momentarily as Red's tongue darted over her ear. She grabbed his face and held it still.

"You know I'm still not gonna call you after this. And you won't see me till I feel like coming back here."

Red brushed his fingers across Kai's mouth.

"Shhhhhhhh," he said and opened his arms.

Kai bit her lip. She pushed her face against his chest and wound her arms around his torso in silence. He folded her in his arms and squeezed her tightly. She could feel the blood racing though her body. Red picked her up and placed her on the edge of the sink. She pulled his shirt up, lightly scratching his chest as she bared his skin. She licked his nipples and whispered her final acquiescence.

"You...bringing...this...on...your...self."

She gasped greedy, sucking breaths as Red nipped at her breasts and unhooked the clasp on her bra. She wanted him inside her, didn't really care for his heavy-handed foreplay, had no interest in sharing the sweetness of lingering kisses with him. She could feel the tingling fullness swelling between her legs and didn't need his touch to coax her body into readiness. As he squeezed her nipples between fumbling fingers, she waited. Returned kisses and waited. Ran her hands up the muscles in his back, let her breath stutter in her chest as heat swelled in the small, dirty, bar restroom. Dug her fingernails into his skin and waited. As he mashed against her clitoris with the force of a wrecking ball, she waited. When she couldn't wait anymore, she unbuckled his pants and reached inside his boxers. She wrapped her hand around his flesh, which was already hard, and massaged and jerked until she could feel it grow in length and width.

They both jumped when a pounding sound vibrated from the door.

"Someone's in here!" Kai yelled.

In the silence she kissed Red on the cheek and opened her hand.

"Where is it?" she asked.

"What?"

"The condom?"

"Oh." He motioned to his back pocket.

Kai reached around him, searching for the small packet. It was there as he had promised. With his tongue tickling her hip, Kai ripped open the wrapper of the condom with fingers and teeth. She pushed him away from her waist. He stood, arching his pelvis forward, as she rolled the condom onto his penis. It only went on halfway; Kai arched an eyebrow in anticipation.

Red pulled her off the sink and guided her to the wall. She

put her hands up and fell forward, the force of him hastening her movements. He lifted the hem of her long jean skirt and gathered it around her waist. She heard a moan rush from his throat. She could almost feel his eyes lingering over the round, fleshy curves of her bare buttocks.

"No underwear, Kai?" he whispered.

She didn't answer. Instead she backed into him, rubbing herself all over his pelvis. He pushed her back to the wall. He bent his knees and nestled his penis between her legs. She tilted her pelvis back and rocked him inside of her. She felt his hand grasp her shoulder, the other hold her waist. They rocked, jerked, and glided themselves sweaty. As Kai felt her breath, her energy, her pleasure ascending, she heard banging at the door again.

"One minute," Kai whispered so low that only Red could hear her. Then she yelled it. "One minute!"

The pounding on the door stilled.

"I want you spread out," Red was whispering as they banged themselves into a frenzy. "I want to be on top of you."

His words went straight to her gut. Kai remembered what it was like to be spread out, remembered how she couldn't breathe when he got close to orgasm. The force of him, fully aroused, about to explode, pushing his all as deep into her as he could. Suddenly, it was swelling inside her—the memories of the all-night-till-morning session from two weeks ago, the pounding on the door, the present madness she and Red were stirring up—and she began to tremble. An orgasmic seam of pleasure opened up inside her pelvis and shot through her body. It came out in an involuntary burst of breath and sound as she felt sweet satiety seep into her muscles. She felt Red shivering behind her and heard his vibrating moan. Then the banging started again.

"We're coming!" she yelled, then covered her mouth. "Now they know it's more than just me in here," she giggled.

She rested her head on the wall to catch her breath as Red let out a postorgasmic groan. Once his breath slowed, he wrapped her arms around Kai and held her tight. He pressed his lips against the nape of her neck and rocked her.

"Red," Kai whispered. "Red, we have to...."

"I can't believe you don't want to see me," he whispered.

"Red, come on, come out of me, we have to go."

"I'm not letting you go, Kai. You have to come home with me. We can't leave it like this. Come, sleep with me."

Kai wriggled in Red's arms, refusing to address his invitation.

"Come on, let me wash up. We'll talk about it at the bar."

Red eased himself out of Kai and released her from his arms. She went over to the sink and turned on the water. She wet a few paper towels and wiped between her legs. She kept her eyes lowered as she rolled her skirt back down to her ankles and adjusted her clothing. She heard Red pulling up his underwear and zipping his pants as she splashed water on her face and dried it on the bottom of her shirt. As she was smoothing her eyebrows, she caught Red standing behind her, staring at her reflection in the mirror.

"Kai, please," he whispered softly.

Kai paused, lost in the intensity of his stare. When the banging erupted again, neither one of them responded. They stood still, caught in the stubborn reflections of each other's eyes.

Rendezvous
D. H. Brent

He was standing in the vegetable section squeezing the peaches when he noticed her. She strolled down the aisle past him, and her scent filled his nose. He savored the sexiness of her perfume—a scent he had not encountered. He was aroused as he took in the curve of her hips, swaying to their own music. She didn't seem to notice him. She picked up a box of fresh strawberries and inhaled their aroma. The sensuous gesture made him want to know more about her. His eyes followed her through the vegetable section until she turned the corner. He turned the corner just in time to see her heading for the checkout counter.

He watched her as she put her items on the counter with graceful, well-manicured hands. A thin gold band encircled the ring finger of her left hand. He walked over and looked through the magazines at the front of the store. He watched her from his secret vantage point as she placed her items on the checkout counter. He looked up from a magazine just as she pushed her cart past him and out the door. He left the magazine rack and followed her outside.

"Can I help you with those?"

She smiled and lifted the bags from the cart. "Thanks, but they're not very heavy." She put the bags on her passenger seat and walked around the car. He followed close behind her, so close that he could smell the oranges in her bag.

"Let me get the door."

She stepped back and let him open the door. Then she walked in front of him, sat down, and slung her shapely legs into the car.

"Here's my number. You can call me anytime," he said through a smile of perfectly aligned teeth. "But I'd like to have yours, too."

She took the business card with the home telephone number scribbled on back and put it in one of the grocery bags.

"I don't have a number," she said as she pulled the door shut.

He stood looking at her as she backed out of the parking space and cruised out of the parking lot.

Two weeks passed and he thought he'd never hear from her. Her scent came back to him sometimes, and he felt the familiar stirring in his pants. He'd gone back to the store where he first saw her, hoping to bump into her again. She never appeared.

I guess some things aren't meant to be, he told himself when she crossed his mind. He'd just have to settle for the occasional daydreams. He was between women right now, and the images he conjured of her while masturbating made his climax more intense. In some way, he felt he already knew her intimately. All he needed was an opportunity to explore her statuesque body.

Two months later, his phone rang. When she asked to speak to John Miller, he attempted to stifle the smile that spread across his mahogany face. Over the static in the line, he asked, "How are you doing?"

She sighed, but didn't answer his question. Instead, she responded with a question of her own. "Can you meet me at the Mark Hotel?"

He tried to hide his excitement. "What?"

"Can you meet me at the Mark Hotel? I'm in Room 613."

"I'll be there in forty-five minutes," John said as he hung up the phone and headed out the door.

She hung up the phone, and sat on the floor nibbling fruit and sipping sherry. The combination always made her horny. She relaxed for a few minutes and went into the bathroom. She touched up her lipstick and slipped out of her robe. The nipples of her full breasts seemed to anticipate her newest conquest. She put on a lace bustier and matching thong, and slowly pulled the red silk slip dress over her head. She stepped into her heels and walked into the living room of the suite.

She was gazing at herself in the full-length mirror when he knocked at the door. She took her time answering. When she opened the door, she could see that he was confident. She liked that. She invited him in and kissed him hard on the lips. He pulled her to him. When she felt the bulge in his pants, she took a step back. "Would you like a drink?" she asked.

"Sure, how about a scotch on the rocks?"

She fixed the drink and set it in front of him. He unbuttoned the collar of his shirt and took a sip of his drink. It was just the way he liked it—good scotch, too. He complimented her on her drink-making skills. She smiled a "thank you" and he wondered about what other skills he would experience tonight.

She crossed her legs and watched him. She could almost see the fiery liquid flow through his muscular body. He reached out to touch her, and she got up and walked over to the window. She stood with her back to him.

"Why did you invite me here?" he asked.

"I was bored."

"You were bored, and you invite a stranger to meet you in your hotel room?"

"Yes."

"Do you do this often?"

"Absolutely."

"I thought you were married."

She turned to face him. "I never said I was married, but would that matter to you?"

"I guess not."

"Maybe this was a bad idea. After you finish your drink, why don't you leave," she said and turned her back to him.

He put his drink down and walked over to her. She turned to face him. She was smiling.

He slapped her face.

Surprised, she reached for the spot and rubbed it. She was pleased. This was more to her liking. She stepped closer to him and grabbed his crotch. "You've got balls. That turns me on."

He pushed her hand away. He didn't want her to feel his rising erection. He was turned on, too.

"What kind of game is this?" he asked.

"Game? This isn't a game. I thought you were leaving."

He pushed past her and walked out the door. In a few moments he had reached his car, whose hood was still warm. He smiled to himself as he slid into the driver's seat. His erection was still intact as he sped out of the hotel parking lot. He was asking himself, "How could I be so wrong?" when he saw the red lights flashing behind him. "Damn." He looked down at the speedometer and saw that he was doing seventy. How the hell was he going to talk his way out of this one?

Fortunately, the police officer was female. As she walked toward his car, he checked her out in his rear view mirror. He could see through her uniform that she was fine. He wondered what made her work at such a lousy job. "Sir, were you aware you were going seventy in a forty-five-mile-an-hour zone?"

John looked at her. "I didn't realize I was speeding, officer. My girlfriend just dumped me, and my head's not on straight. Forgive me?"

She seemed to soften her stance. He noticed the way she gazed at him as she looked down into the car. Inspecting his body from head to crotch with her hazel eyes, she said, "I still need to see your license." He reached into his back pocket to retrieve his wallet, and she stood looking at him with a sensuous smile. He handed her his license and stroked her hand as she pulled it away. She walked back to her cruiser, thinking, *Fine as you are, your girlfriend just dumped you?*

After a few minutes, she came back to his car. "You don't have any warrants or outstanding tickets, so this time I'll give you a warning," she said. "But I'll be keeping my eyes on you, Mr. Miller. Take care of that broken heart."

"Thanks, officer." He watched her ass in the rearview mirror as she walked back to her cruiser. He smiled as he pulled away from the curb, and drove the speed limit the rest of the way home. He poured himself a stiff drink as soon as he walked through the door. "The nerve of that woman!" he said aloud. "*I've* got balls? She's a ball-bustin' freak." He sat down and turned on the TV. He flipped through the channels and fell asleep in his expensive clothes—drink still in his hand. She rode him in his dreams, and he awoke at four A.M. with a hard-on.

Weeks passed and she continued to creep into his thoughts at the damnedest times, but he always brushed her aside. He tried not to think about her when he masturbated. It seemed that masturbation was becoming a way of life for him.

It took a while, but he finally got her out of his mind. Even though he wasn't looking for a serious relationship, he had been out on a few dates. Friends and family always had somebody they wanted him to meet. A few of the sisters he had gone out with were fine, and actually seemed to have their lives together.

He was reviewing the financials for tomorrow's breakfast meeting when the phone rang. "Meet me at the downtown Hilton, Room 1252."

"What kind of bulls—?" The phone went dead in his hand.

He walked over to the refrigerator and opened a beer. He took a gulp and went into the bathroom. He showered and shaved. *I may be crazy, but if I don't go over there, I'll never know,* he told himself as he pulled on a silk shirt and crisply creased pants. He ran his fingers through his close-cropped hair and splashed on some after-shave before walking out the door.

He knocked on the door of Room 1252, and it opened. He slowly walked inside. The lights were turned down. He took in the large suite, which was permeated with her scent. There was a scotch on the rocks sitting on the table in front of him. He took a sip and sat down. She wasn't in the living room of the suite. It occurred to him that he didn't even know her name. "Guess this is another one of those sick games," he muttered to himself. "I'm gonna drink up and get out of here."

As he stood up to leave, she came through the door. He sat back down. "Sorry to keep you waiting, but I had to pick up a few things." She went to him and sat in his lap. She kissed him slowly, moving her tongue in and out of his mouth. As their tongues danced together, she moved her ass around in his lap. He grabbed her hair and pulled her head back. Kissing her neck, he started to move his tongue down the open collar of her coat.

She stood up and took off her coat. She was naked. He reached for her and she stepped back.

"You're beautiful. But you know that, don't you?"

She didn't answer.

She went to the bar and poured herself a drink.

She walked back over to him and took a sip.

Then, she poured the rest of the drink across her breasts.

He watched the brown liquid slide down her breasts and over her flat stomach. She slid her hand over her stomach and reached her fingers inside.

"Don't you want to taste it?"

He walked over to her. He circled her nipples with his finger and licked them.

"Tastes good. But you know that too, don't you?"

He squeezed her breasts together and leaned down to suck her nipples. He licked her breasts and her stomach until the sherry was gone. She tore his shirt open and moved her hands over his chest. She played with his nipples and kissed him again. She fell on her knees and unzipped his pants. She took his dick in her warm hands and squeezed it softly. She kneaded him until he became stiff, admiring the glistening mahogany skin in the dim light. She kissed his dick and circled the tip with her tongue. Slowly she took him in her mouth and sucked until he moaned. "It's beautiful," she whispered, looking up into his handsome face.

She continued to stroke him with her hand. He moaned and grabbed her head. He moved back and forth in her mouth. He knew his first orgasm was not far off. "Damn, that feels good," he said through clenched teeth. "Don't stop! I'm almost there."

She got up and walked into the bedroom. He followed her. Just as he approached, she closed the door. He heard the lock turn. He stood there in disbelief. "I'll call you," she said through the door.

He finished his drink, and sat down in the chair and shook his head. His dick was still throbbing. He touched himself. He stroked his hard dick. It felt good, and damn, he needed a release. He stroked it harder, faster. He closed his eyes and imagined she was still on her knees in front of him. He imagined that his hand was her warm, full-lipped mouth. He continued to stroke and soon he was jerking off. Spurts of his juices landed on his Allen Edmonds shoes and Hugo Boss pants. He didn't notice, though. He immersed himself in the release and was surprised by the shudder his body gave as the last of his hot liquid spread over his hand. He moaned and sat back in the chair. After the euphoria passed, he opened his eyes and stood up. He walked over to the bar to wash his hands.

"You're good at that," she said as she came up behind him. "Here, let me do that for you."

She took his arm and turned him around to face her. He glared at her, and his jaw pulsed with the fury he felt. He kept his hands still so that he wouldn't grab her neck and shake her until she was lifeless.

She took his hand and raised it to her mouth. She slowly sucked his juices from his fingers. "You taste good," she said. She kept her eyes on him as she licked his palm.

He reached for his zipper. She put her hand on his to stop him from zipping up his pants. She knelt down and took his now-spent dick into her mouth. She slowly sucked and licked, sucked and licked. He fought the urge to give into her, but his manhood had a different agenda. He gave into her.

"I want you. Why don't you give me some of the pleasure you gave yourself?" she asked.

He didn't answer. He just stood looking at her.

She lay back on the floor and spread her legs. She licked her fingers and circled her nipples—they jumped to attention. She licked her fingers again and played with her clit. She looked at him and smiled. Sliding her fingers inside her trim pussy, she moved her broad hips slowly. He could hear her fingers moving in and out of her juicy hole. The sound made him want to plunge inside her, but he stood still. She continued masturbating, and he could see the juices oozing out of her pussy. She arched her back and moaned. She licked her fingers and smiled at him. "Tastes good," she giggled.

He knelt in front of her and kissed her stomach. He slowly

licked her thighs. He moved his mouth to her mound and kissed it. She lay back and he darted his tongue in and out of her pussy. He sucked her clit and put his fingers inside her. She moved to the rhythm of his fingers, and another orgasm spread over his thick fingers. He continued fingering her until she came again. She panted and moaned, moaned and panted. She clutched for his head. He looked at the rise and fall of her breasts. He leaned over her and sucked her nipples. She was writhing under him. "Turn over," he said.

He licked the juices from her, and massaged her ass with his large hands. He ran his tongue over her ass and kissed it. He smacked her ass a few times and licked some more. She moved her hips back and forth. He could see that her opening was throbbing. She was ready.

"I want you so damned bad," she moaned.

He stood up, and looked down at her. Damn, she was beautiful. He ran his fingers through his hair. "Call me," he said as he walked toward the door.

She lay there a moment—not believing he would walk away from this moment, from her. She jumped up and ran to the door. She looked down the hall, but he was already gone.

The Christening
Shawn E. Rhea

It had taken nearly six months, but Kevin's house was finally in order. It felt good to walk through the door this time and not be greeted by a barrage of boxes and bare walls. He set down his suitcase, swiped a week's worth of mail off the floor, and headed for his den. Once there, he plopped down on the couch and sank into its plush suede cushions.

The week had been a rough one. Kevin's firm had assigned him to head up the audit of the municipal books of Canton, Ohio. The city was supposed to have a surplus, but somehow the money had disappeared and the new mayor intended to find out where it had gone. Kevin, together with his team of accountants, had to do more than a little arm twisting and threatening to get straight answers from department managers about some of the city's expenditures. But they had finally gotten the information, and now a few folks had some serious explaining to do. He was scheduled to be back in Canton first thing Monday morning, and the shit he was wading through only promised to get deeper. But it was Friday, and he at least had the weekend to recharge his battery.

"Bills...credit card offers...refinance your mortgage...more junk," Kevin mumbled to himself as he sorted through his mail and vaguely considered what he could get into for the weekend. He didn't know Detroit that well. He hadn't even wanted to move to the city, but the promotion was too good to pass up. His accounting firm kept the books for a number of major municipalities, and for the past six years he had been moving city-to-city, working on whatever audit team was in need of his expertise. He had developed a reputation for weeding out waste, and it had finally gotten him a major salary increase and a promotion to Midwest manager. He was supervising audits in ten different cities, and Detroit, where his company had a satellite office, was his base.

He hated leaving Atlanta. He loved its warm weather and abundance of beautiful black women. The vibe and pulse of a steamy summer night there—the trees budding with peach blossoms, bare-legged sistas in skimpy sun dresses—was enough to give him an erection just thinking about it. Detroit, on the other hand, had a ridiculously short summer, and in the winter it was too cold to get out much. Besides, Kevin hated driving in the snow. He was a born and bred southern boy with an accent, courtesy of New Orleans, to prove it.

But his hellish week was making him determined to get out and blow off some steam over the weekend. Tamara offered to come visit him from Atlanta, but Kevin managed to squirm his way out of it. Now he was kicking himself. It had been nearly a month since he'd fucked, and hand jobs just weren't cutting it. What he needed was some good old-fashioned pussy. It had always been good with Tamara, but it was all the other stuff that came along with their relationship that he could no longer handle. She was a beautiful woman. Smart. Sexy as all hell, but he just wasn't ready to give her what he knew she wanted and deserved. She had started hinting about a year ago that marriage and babies were on her list of priorities. Not that Kevin was totally opposed to getting married and having children. At thirty-six he certainly was old enough and set up enough to handle the responsibility. It's just that the timing was all wrong. He never knew when his company was going to move him. He had only been in Atlanta for two years and that was longer than he'd been in any of the other six cities that they'd shipped him off to. He just didn't think it was fair to ask a woman to uproot her life and give up her career every time Caper & Chaney decided to send him somewhere.

In that regard the move to Detroit had been a good thing. It had put some distance between him and Tamara, and finally the relationship was beginning to peter out. He knew that it was hurting her, and he knew that she was hoping her visit might help them find their way back to each other. But he just wouldn't give her any false hope. That would be even crueler. Kevin had put Tamara off for months now, saying that his house was still a mess, still filled with boxes sitting in the middle of his floor. It hadn't been a lie, but it also wasn't the truth of why he didn't want her to visit. He had visited her several times in Atlanta since his move, but some part of him wanted to keep his new home a Tamara-free zone. Now it had been nearly a month since they'd been together, however, and he was beginning to get a little crazy.

Kevin tossed the mail on top of the coffee table and headed over to the phone to check his messages. He hit the caller ID button and paged through the numbers: his mom; his boy, Lance; the dry cleaners—probably reminding him to pick up his shirts—and Char Westin. "Char Westin," Kevin said out loud. A sly smile crept over his face. Maybe the weekend was looking up after all.

Char Westin was a writer for the city's weekly newspaper. It was a liberal rag that survived mostly on personal ads and club listings, but threw in enough political coverage to make itself legitimate. Char was an investigative reporter, but she had told him her real love was fiction and essay writing. She'd had several pieces anthologized and now her agent was shopping a collection of her work around to the publishing houses. "I may never get rich doing this shit, but I love my work," she'd told Kevin that first night they were introduced by Lance at his birthday party.

On the surface they were total opposites. Kevin, with his clean-cut looks and button-down shirts, was much more practical than Char. He truly couldn't understand why anyone would choose a profession that didn't promise a fat bank account. Char, by contrast, admitted that she sometimes went weeks without balancing her checkbook. Normally a revelation like that would have made Kevin write a woman off as an airhead and sent him scrambling to the other end of the party looking for the bar. But there was something about Char Westin. Something in the tone of her voice, something in the way she could break down the political dynamics of Arab- and African-American relations in Detroit—a city that had a large population of both groups—that told him she was far from being an airhead. And besides, the girl had a high, tight ass that could seriously fill out a pair of jeans, and intense eyes that hinted at secrets that would only be revealed in private. So he stayed and he talked to her.

Kevin had taken Char out for the first time just about a month ago. They had gone to a reggae club—not something that Kevin would normally have opted to do. He was more of a jazz man himself. But she had insisted, and Kevin had not had a chance to check out much of Detroit, so it wasn't as if he had a list of spots to hit. *What the hell,* he thought when she suggested that they go.

The club was thick with the scent of reefer, a smell he had never particularly cared for. But he quickly forgot his disdain once Char took off her ski jacket. She was wearing a pair of tight black pants that just covered the upper curve of her ass. There was a rhinestone navel ring peeking out from her belly button. It was the dead of winter but she was wearing a black tank top. Char handed her jacket to the coat check attendant, then turned toward Kevin. He quickly averted his eyes away from the direction of her lower extremities. It was too late, though. She had seen him. "Oh, you'll see in a minute why I dressed like this. It's very warm in there," she said unapologetically. She smiled, waited for him to check his coat, then grabbed his hand and led him into the club.

Char had been right. Even for a southern boy it was uncomfortably warm in the club. Red and green lights illuminated the cramped dance floor. Kevin, with his pressed corduroys and hairless face, felt slightly out of place in a club full of dreadlocks and low-slung, baggy jeans. Young women with braids, locks, and afros were in back-bending positions, winding against their partners, riding their pelvises, seemingly holding on for dear life.

"So, what do you think?" Char asked him. She touched his arm and positioned her body right in front of him. Even in the dark he was aware of her eyes staring into his, hinting at those secrets that he was dying to hear, touch, taste.

"It's cool," he said, smiling.

She took his hand and began a slow wind to the music's rhythm. Kevin tried to mimic her moves, but he had never been much of a dancer. She moved her hands down toward his hips and attempted to loosen up his wind. Kevin laughed at his own stiffness—both the one in his hips and the other one growing in another part of his body. He tried to follow her lead, but he only managed more movement from his legs. Nothing from his hips.

"It starts here," Char explained, placing a hand over his heart, "and travels down here"—now she was moving her ring-adorned finger down the center of his torso—"and explodes right here," she finished, gripping both hands around his hips again.

"I'm tryin', I'm tryin'," he insisted.

They danced through one more song before Kevin suggested that they hit the bar for a drink. "Red Stripe," he ordered.

"I'll have a shot of Cuervo on the rocks with a lime."

Char took a sip from her drink. "So tell me, Kevin Ashby, how do you like Detroit so far?"

"To tell you the truth, I'm not feelin' it too much."

"I know what you mean. This can be a hard city if you don't know people. I grew up here, and coming back and reconnecting with folks has been a major adjustment."

"Well, I've been traveling for my job so much that I really haven't had a chance to make the effort. But how exactly does a brotha connect with folks around here?"

"Well, you've already made one important connection," Char said, looking him dead in his eyes and taking another sip from her drink.

She was using those intense eyes to flirt with him. They were power and she knew it. They were a challenge, saying, *Can you step up?* He damn sure could. He stared back, placed his hand on her knee, and moved toward her face. "And that would be you, I take it?" He added a devilish smile for emphasis.

"But of course. There are things I could show you."

"What things?"

"Some things are better experienced than told." With that Char threw back the rest of her tequila, stepped up from the bar, and dragged him off toward the dance floor.

They were sweaty and about seven sheets to the wind apiece by the time they left the club. Kevin's hips were decidedly looser, and he had nearly mastered a slow wind.

"Not bad for a buttoned-up corporate boy," Char joked as she slid into the passenger side of his SUV.

"Are you implying that I'm a little stiff?" Kevin countered, mocking a tone of disbelief.

"Me? Never."

Kevin laughed, turned the ignition key, and began angling the car out of the club's makeshift parking lot. "I had a nice time tonight. Next time, I'll have to take you to check out some jazz, so you can get a sense of how I flow."

"Actually, I've got a pretty decent jazz collection myself. Maybe you can come by and check it out."

"I'd love to do that one evening."

"How 'bout *this* evening?"

And there it was: the offer that had gotten him as close to some local pussy as he'd gotten since moving to Detroit. "Yeah, that sounds cool." Kevin accepted before she had a chance to change her mind.

Her apartment was awash in earth tones, and a large bank of windows looked out over downtown and the river. Char put a CD into the stereo, lit a few candles, and turned off the lights.

"Ah, George Benson's 'White Rabbit,'" remarked Kevin as the first notes of Alan Rubin's horn sounded, followed by Benson's Spanish-inflected guitar picking.

"Very good." She joined him on the window seat and spent a few minutes pointing out some nearby attractions: the casino, the GM building, Eastern Market. They could spy people moving around in the twin tower apartment building directly across the way. The thought of being watched by others brought a rise to Kevin's pants. He wanted to lay Char down and fuck her right there on the window seat, in plain view of several hundred other residents. He moved in and kissed her on her lips. Softly first. Barely a graze. Then he placed his hand on her face and firmly pulled her toward him. The kiss was building now. He was exploring the fullness of her lips; the warm, slow groove of her tongue; its soft underside. Now his hands were underneath her tank top, and he could feel hers skimming the area just below his navel and above his quickly stiffening dick. Char unzipped his pants and slid her hand inside his boxer shorts. She moved her fingers through his pre-cum and began softly rimming the tip of his engorged cock.

Kevin buried his head into the nape of Char's neck. He could smell the faint residue of her perfume. She smelled of vanilla and amber. His tongue licked her neck and he could taste the salt left on her body from their evening of dancing. He badly wanted to fuck her, and he knew she wanted him too, but something stopped him. Tamara. Kevin was leaving the next morning to visit her in Atlanta, and he was finally going to break things off with her. Tell her that he thought they should date other people. It was going to be hard enough, and he didn't need the guilt of fucking another woman on his mind.

He pulled back and looked into Char's eyes. He could see her secrets ready to spill forth, and he strongly wanted to become acquainted with them. He wanted to know the sound of her voice when she came and the scream rose from deep within her groin. He wanted to feel the tightening and contracting of her pussy around his dick. He wanted to know the slickness of her when she rode him. But he wanted to know it without reservations.

"What's wrong?" she asked.

"Nothing," he lied. "It's just that I have to get up really early in the morning to catch a flight and if we start this I won't want to leave."

"Oh, I understand."

She smiled and pulled her hands out of his pants. She clasped her fingers around his, dropped her head, and let out a frustrated but resigned laugh. Kevin joined her. When they finished laughing, he lifted her chin with his hand. "But I'd like to give you a little something to think about while I'm traveling," he said. With that, he lay her down on the window seat, shimmied off her pants, and spread her legs. *There's no reason why we both need to be frustrated,* he thought as he softly parted the lips of her pussy. He slid his index finger and thumb along the length of her cunt, then gently massaged the lips. His thumb began a rhythmic ride over her clit, while the middle finger of his other hand found its way inside her vagina. Char's breathing was becoming more audible now, and she inhaled at a quicker pace. She arched her back, then turned her head to look out the window. Kevin looked too. He could see people over in the other apartments. Some were moving around, others were sitting, but he couldn't tell if anyone actually saw them.

He stuck two more fingers inside Char and she began to ride him fiercely now. He could hear her screams moving up from that deep place. They were guttural and wild. He could feel her juices on his fingers. Her body began to rack with spasm after spasm. "Oh, fuck!" she screamed right as the final wave hit her.

When it was over, Char tightened her thighs around his hands and buried her very satisfied face into the crook of her arm. A second later, when her breathing had returned to normal, she sat up, took his face into her hands, and softly kissed him on the lips.

"That was incredible," she said. "Very generous. I can't wait to return the favor."

Kevin stood up, and Char shimmied back into her pants. He grabbed his coat off the couch, gave her a final kiss, and promised to call her when he got back from Atlanta. He had to jack off that night just to get to sleep. He drifted off inhaling the mingled scent of both their bodies on his hand.

Even after Kevin showered and dressed the next morning, the smell of Char stayed with him. He was certain that once he reached Atlanta Tamara would hug him, take one whiff of his skin, and know instinctively what he had come to tell her: that they both needed to move on, that he had already begun the journey. But if Tamara knew she did not let on, so the weekend had been one big exercise in denial for Kevin. For two days he laughed at all the right moments, stared longingly into Tamara's eyes when they made love, and played the committed boyfriend while they were together with mutual friends. He willfully beat back any surfacing feelings of guilt whenever he thought about how he planned to break the news to Tamara just before she took him to the airport on Sunday. *No need to ruin the weekend,* he kept telling himself.

She cried when he told her it was over, and Kevin said "no" when she asked if he had met another woman. "I'm simply not prepared to change my life the way you need me to," he said before kissing her cheek and brushing a tear-soaked strand of hair from her eye. His answer was not exactly a lie. Kevin had made up his mind to end things long before he met Char. But he had thought of her often, too often, even while making love to Tamara.

He called Char the Wednesday after he returned from Atlanta. The message on her home machine said she'd be out of town for a week on assignment. Between her story deadlines and his business travel they had been playing telephone tag and taking rain checks for nearly a month now, neither of their schedules jibing with the others. Kevin had given up hope that they would ever hook up, but now her name had shown up on his caller ID. He dialed his voicemail and paged through the messages until he reached hers.

"Hello, You, this is Char. We seem to be having the damndest time catching up with each other, but I thought I'd call on the off chance that you are going to be around this weekend. Maybe we can get together and I can repay that favor I owe you. Give me a call if you'd like to."

Kevin hung up the receiver and smiled. He looked around

the room and nodded his head in approval of the way his house had come together. It was finally beginning to feel like home. All it needed was an official christening. He walked into the kitchen, pulled two bottles of champagne from the wine rack, and stuck them into the refrigerator to chill. He picked up the phone and dialed Char's number.

"Hello?" a voice answered.

"Char?"

"Yes?"

"This is Kevin. How would you like to help christen my house?"

Seeing Stars
Samiya A. Bashir

Z thought she would never survive the noise. She'd traveled thousands of miles from home to get to the West, to America, to New York City, and absorbing the crisp, piquant language was not a problem. She'd been well warned of the cold, and while it was worse than she could have imagined, she'd at least felt prepared. Even the immensity of so many different kinds of faces flying super-speed all around her wasn't as unsettling as the unremitting brightness—and the noise.

The first words she said to her aunt, T, after the greetings, hugs and kisses, exchange of news, were: *These people, they must be very afraid of the dark.* Her aunt laughed; her young American cousins shook their heads, not getting the joke. After sitting for hours with immigration, they carted her trunk and bags, heavy with gifts, to the car. She was quiet for most of the ride into Brooklyn, jaw dropped as she tried to take everything in.

Pictures were no match for the enormity of everything around her. Z could see the lights of the Empire State Building in the distance, but her attention was broken each time she tried to stare by the constant darting of cars in and out of the traffic around them. The road was huge. The cars were huge. The people in the cars were huge. The sky, a bright gray, was huge; but no matter how hard she tried to block out everything around her, Z couldn't find a single star.

The electricity in the air was so heavy she could feel it. Her first nights in the city, it seemed as if the sun never set. She was nauseated, the hairs on her arms and the back of her neck stood straight. The lights never dimmed enough for her to find her favorite stars, the touchstones that would keep her from feeling too far from home. Z was shaken by the omen she saw in the sky. Her mother, her grandmother, her sisters were in hiding behind the manufactured light, and she knew they were out there reaching toward her. But this new place spun like a sparkling force field erected to keep her from feeling safe.

Her aunt had thankfully given Z a week to get acclimated before she started the job that had been arranged for her. T was a nurse at the hospital and had arranged for her niece to work in maintenance while she attended school. That week, she mostly lay in her room, reaching for quiet. Giving up, she sometimes watched television with her cousins. They took her out to see some of the sights once, but she became overwhelmed by the quickness of everything. Fast walking, fast talking, fast driving. The bicyclists rode as if they were racing. Fifty-foot televisions blared from the sides of buildings. Her cousins teased her for her skittishness.

Z found a patch of grass, a couple of blocks from the house, where she spent afternoons just listening to people talk. She was wooed by the different languages and looks black people had here. Some looked like they were from back home, but when they opened their mouths they sounded like everyone else. Each night she sat at her window and looked for her stars. She found one on the second night. A few nights later she saw a few more, but there were never more than a tiny handful fighting through the bright night sky.

Once she started work, she had less time for reflection. She worked the graveyard shift at first, but picked up as many doubles as she could. She liked the people she worked with, and found herself daydreaming over the rhythmic pull of the mop over the floor. While the paper towel wiped cleanser off of windows and counters, she grew her English by listening to the television dramas playing full blast in every patient's room. Z picked up pieces from people talking all around her and found comfort in knowing she wasn't alone in her struggle to communicate.

On the long days when she stayed over for an afternoon shift, Z was kept awake by Reagan, a young orderly who kept her in stitches with tales of her wild life. Through Reagan, Z learned about things like pantylines and body shots, rave parties, shotgun tokes, hip-hop concerts, wonder bras, and the best quiet spots in the library to read both alone and with someone else. Reagan was two years younger than Z but lived on her own. Although she moved to the city to be a singer, Reagan still hadn't sung much outside of karaoke bars and back alleyways.

Z loved listening to Reagan talk and scheduled as many afternoon double shifts as she could. She needed the money; she was still repaying her aunt for the airfare she borrowed to get here. But more than that, hanging out with Reagan was a periodic cure for the loneliness that dragged behind her like September storm clouds. Z felt completely out of place here, in this jungle, where everyone else seemed so wild and free. She didn't have a thing in common with her own cousins. They were still just kids, and their big concerns were school and those video games they played all day and night. They had only been back home once, and couldn't imagine life without television or a million grams of sugar a day.

She was in no hurry to be rushed into marriage, like her aunt's friends would have her do. She had come to go to school, to try to make a new life. Even if Z wasn't sure what that meant yet, she was beginning to get an idea. She started going for long walks, sometimes even walking to and from work. She would look around at the houses and the people, pass by the restaurants and sidewalk cafés. In the park large groups of men played football, just like back home.

Over the months, Z slowly started to relax into her new environment. She was comfortable with her job. She had repaid her aunt, and was sending money home to her mother and sisters. She was also saving money to start school and had even begun going out to movies and parties with Reagan. Usually she just sat in the corner and watched everything that went on. Sometimes people would come and talk to her, but she was so shy she didn't quite know what to say. Z felt as if she was carrying a big secret that no one here—no one who wasn't from home—would understand.

Reagan pushed her to go on dates, but Z always playfully changed the subject. One afternoon they decided to have lunch together in the park by the hospital. Reagan spread out a sheet she'd copped from the supply closet, and they lay down and spread out their food. Reagan was midway through the dramatic story of her date last night with one ex when another showed up at the same party.

Now, you remember that Dylan dumped me because I was cheating on him with Shakira? That was, like, a year ago, but we talked it all out. You remember, I told you about it a few weeks ago, how we sat up all night watching the Twilight Zone *marathon and talked all about our relationship and how we were both responsible for the breakdown in communication—* Z knew it was pointless to try to get a word in once Reagan got going, so she just nodded for her to go on.

Yeah, so I was sitting there having a drink with Dylan,

and we're just talking about this film we went to see—you have got to see it, but I'll tell you in a minute—and in walks Shakira. She's with her new *girlfriend and they both look so totally hot I almost dropped my drink. I stopped talking mid-sentence and just stared. I'm telling you, I totally forgot where I even was and that I was talking, much less what I was supposed to be talking about. And Dylan sees this. And all of Dylan's friends see this. And Dylan gets all pissed and tries to start an argument with me but, like, I'm not trying to have an argument with him, all in front of everybody. Especially not in front of Shakira.*

Reagan thinks about what to say next, just long enough to put a forkful of salad into her mouth, chew it, swallow it, and reach for another. *So anyway, we have to leave and it becomes a big hairy deal, like I was just telling you, until, of course, we wind up in bed having the best sex ever.*

You mean, Z pipes in, *since last week.*

Yeah. Oh wow, yeah. Last week was off the hook. But last night was even better. *I'm telling you. He was so passionate. By the time we got there he was feeling all sorry and apologizing for even getting mad and talking about how grateful he was to have me back with him and all that. You know, kissing my ass just like I like it...and I just really let go.*

They sat quiet for a while after that. Z was trying to imagine what it would feel like to have her ass kissed. Reagan was daydreaming about the sun as it rose over Dylan's sweaty back. She stretched a smile across her face as she remembered how high it had risen by the time they finally went to sleep. *Yeah, Z,* she said with a wink and a smile. *You should've been there.*

Z laughed along with her friend and finished her sandwich. She was just polishing off the last drops of tea from her thermos when she steeled herself to ask the question she'd been holding in for so long. *Reagan?*

Yeah?

I was wondering...could you tell me...I mean...what's it like?

Reagan always seemed a bit amused that Z was a virgin. She got the whole thing about where she was from, and Z'd told her about the arranged marriages and how she wasn't ready for anything like that. Reagan had even tried to get her to go out on dates, offering to double, but Z seemed petrified by the idea of letting anyone close to her. *I mean, there's virgin,* thought Reagan, *and then there's VIRGIN.* Z acted as if she didn't even know what it was like to kiss a guy. Reagan filled her mouth with a huge bite of her sandwich and leaned back on the grass. She was just daydreaming and chewing, daydreaming and chewing with this sneaky, lusty expression on her face that drew Z closer. It was as if she could sniff the excitement radiating from Reagan's body into her own.

When she finished chewing, Reagan swallowed slowly, licking all around her mouth and wiping both lips before she began. *Well, when I'm with a man, I feel like the most extraordinary gift.* She checked Z's face for a reaction, then continued. *I feel wrapped completely in the beautiful paper of his skin. His arms strong around me. His head buried in my neck or planting kisses across my face, my chest, my fingers. The smell of a man gets all over you, Z—inside and through you like a cloud of honor. It feels like he's worshipping me, like somehow I'm worthy of worship. And when I let him inside of me, it's as if I'm returning the favor, enveloping him in my warmth, wrapping him in the flow of my juices.*

I circle my legs and arms around him and draw him closer and closer. And we're both covering each other with kisses now, and burrowing our heads in each other's necks, and when we're both as close as we can possibly be—it's like fireworks. It's the most extraordinary kind of love burst. Yeah. That's it. It feels like it would if you could concentrate all the love in the world into a tight ball that could barely stretch enough to contain it. And once you crammed that last bit of love inside, it burst, and set all the love rushing free again.

They both sat on the grass hugging their knees to their chests. Z sat speechless, trying to imagine. As hard as she tried to paint the picture in her mind, there were holes, blank spaces she couldn't quite fill in. When she could finally stammer out a few words, she turned her face to Reagan and asked, *What about women? When you're with them, is it the same?*

Reagan thought about it for a moment before deciding. *Yes, and no.* Z drew closer, tuning out all distractions with rapt attention. *When I'm with a woman it's like the ultimate acceptance. All the little fears and doubts, the self-consciousness—it all dies away. It's like discovering everything that's beautiful about myself. Not like hearing someone else saying it, but seeing it with your own eyes and knowing it's true. All of that nitpicking fault game I play in the mirror disappears and I'm left awestruck by the soft, delectable beauty in all kinds of bodies. When I'm with a woman, it's like the softest embrace; like being reborn and the world is new and bright and loud and scary, but there is someone holding me through it with comfort and protection, kisses and caresses, sweet, heavy smells and precision.*

It's the most intimate I've ever been with anyone. The most naked, the most fully seen and fully loved and accepted. And—oh—the fireworks. It's like the sky has suddenly burst into a million million stars in a rainbow of colors. That's the difference, really. The stars are no brighter, no more spectacular. The release is no less sweet. It's just that everything is bathed in rich, vibrant color. Yeah...that's it.

Z was trying as hard as she could to imagine it. But she couldn't. She felt close when she remembered lying in the grass with her friends back home, listening to the bees buzz above them. Or the nights she would sneak out to the stream and hold hands with G, or with B, talking about the future when they would all come to America. She felt Reagan watching her and her face went hot. *Have you ever had an orgasm, Z?* Her face grew even hotter as she looked down at her hands and slowly shook her head.

I don't really know. I don't really know what it is.

Well...hell, I don't know. It's like when you're having sex, with yourself or with someone else, and, like...it's that part where the love explodes and you see the stars...all that.

No, said Z. *I told you I've never done that with anyone. I can't until I'm married, anyway.*

Well, said Reagan, painting that sly grin across her cheeks again as she leaned in to whisper, *you* can *do anything you want. You just have* chosen *not to do it until you get married.*

No, said Z, tears welling in her eyes, *I can't. You don't understand,* she said, lying back on the grass. *You can't understand! I must wait until I get married. After a while, I'll have a marriage arranged from home and then I'll do it. No one here would want to take me out, anyway—*

Whoa, there. You can stop right there, 'cause you know that ain't true. Didn't I tell you Ronnie in pediatrics has been sniffin' around after you like a lost dog?

You don't understand, Reagan. Just...believe me. You couldn't understand.

What couldn't I understand? I have crazy, fanatical parents too. I moved away. Now I do what I want. I mean, at least you can get out the vibrator when your aunt's not home. Take advantage of different shifts.... Reagan stopped when she recognized that lost look that spread across Z's face when she didn't understand a particular expression someone said. *I know you know what a vibrator is. My god, you are from* Earth, *Z! They have vibrators everywhere.*

Z just shook her head. She was trying to think of what the word meant, but all she could think of were pagers and cell phones. *OK,* said Reagan, as if she'd just uncovered a major conspiracy or was about to impart a wonderful secret. *A vibrator is, like, a sex toy. You turn it on and it vibrates, like a pager—kind of,* Z nodded, *but stronger and longer. You can rub it all over your body. But then, when you put it down over your clit,* said Reagan, as she lay back and tried to illustrate, *and rub it around, it's just like someone else's finger or mouth or body—only better. 'Cause you control the power with a flick of your thumb.*

Reagan was about thirty seconds into laughing when she realized Z wasn't joining her. Instead, she looked like she was about to start crying again. *Whoa, my humor's not that bad....* Still no smile. *Hey, what's the matter?*

I...I can't do that. Z wished she'd never asked the question. She wanted out of this conversation before Reagan tried to justify how everyone could have a wild and free life like hers. Before she had to explain why Reagan could never understand. *I just...I can't touch that. I can't do that....* Reagan tried to break in, explain how easy it was, how she could even loan her one and show her how to use it, when Z burst out.... *It won't work! It won't work on me, nothing will work on me down there.*

Reagan just watched her friend as she burst into tears. She didn't know what she meant, but knew that it wasn't a good time to push her. *I...I'm not whole like you, Reagan,* Z started, slowly. *Back home...we have a tradition and...I don't have the things you're talking about. I'm not like you. I can't feel that explosion or see the stars and colors like you see, Reagan. Just...please just leave me alone about this. OK?*

Wait a minute, Z...are you talking about.... Z just nodded her head. *All of it?* Z nodded again.

I mean, Z started, searching for the right words. *I mean, there is still some little opening. They had to cut it when I started bleeding. But they removed the top and...and sewed it so that there would be no feeling. No pain. No joy. When*

I get married, my husband will open me fully and I will hope that I heal enough in time to have babies so there will be no problems. Z started to trail off, daring herself to look her friend in the eye. *It's a badge of honor back home. All the girls do it. They prepare us our whole lives for this, this amazing transition. But they don't really tell us what it is. None of us really knew what it was until they did it to us. I'm the only one who tried to run away when I saw what they were doing. My friends were so strong.*

Z was wiping the tears from her cheeks as fast as they fell, wanting to get these words out while she had the courage. She needed to tell someone, get the weight of her secret off her chest. *They thought they could shame me—my friends, my family—for fighting. For trying to get away, for shouting and saying out loud I wish they had never touched me. I wished they had left me alone. My mother said I brought shame on the family with my words. She said no man would marry me if I didn't transition into a proper woman. But there was no shame they could give me stronger than what I carried. I felt...ripped apart. Torn to shreds. I couldn't understand how* this *is what would make someone want to love me. Whenever I looked at what they'd done, all I could feel was shame. How would anyone ever want to love...that?*

Z turned to pack up her lunch until she was ready to read the horror on her friend's face. She knew how women in America felt about what happened back home. How they thought her people were barbaric, the women stupid. She was ready to say good-bye to the lunches and the fun stories Reagan shared with her, but when she looked into her friend's eyes she couldn't find any pity. Reagan scooted over and gave Z a quick hug, sat back, and shrugged her shoulders.

All right then, she said matter-of-factly. *So that's done. That doesn't mean you can't feel good. It certainly doesn't mean no one will love you or want to date you. But we can worry about that later. Right now it's all about the* big O. Reagan smiled so brightly, and Z was so shocked, that she had no choice but to join her. She was just about to argue with her friend when Reagan continued, *There are a thousand places on your body that respond to touch, Z. The clit rocks, for sure, don't get me wrong. But still, I accept no excuses for an orgasm-free existence. You're beautiful, all you've got to do is what women have done forever, honey...use what you've got! Come on...I'll tell you more after work. I'm takin' you out! Let's get back before we catch an earful.*

Reagan and Z went out after work, sleeplessness and delirium mixed with the freedom Z felt having shared her secret. It was a perfectly clear night. Z counted exactly twenty-three stars, the most she'd seen since she arrived. Reagan plied Z with food and dessert while telling her story after story of her journey through self-love. Z learned about the first time Reagan did it, pulling down her Spiderman Underoos after her parents tucked her in and turned off the lights. Z remembered playing with herself in the dark when she was a little girl: how sweet the pleasure was, how she knew instinctively to keep quiet so as not to wake anyone else in the house.

As the night progressed, Reagan told Z all about vibrators and dildos, gels and lubes, powders and feathers, whips and chains, and rubbers and ropes. Z got home exhausted, thinking about the miracles that could be attained from just the right pressure on a nipple, or the pinching of a thigh. She gave cursory greetings to her cousins, said goodnight to her aunt, and fell into bed. Her dreams were filled with lips and tongues, probing fingers, and taut, sensitive skin.

When she awoke late the next morning the house was eerily silent. Her aunt had left for work over an hour ago; her cousins had gone to school. She wasn't due at work until late that night, and had the house to herself for the rest of the day.

She rolled over and tried to climb back into the wet warmth of the dream she'd been having, but it was too late. She was up.

Images of laundry, dishes, and the dinner that needed to be prepared before everyone came home poked around her mind but she shooed them away. Instead, her fingers began slowly trailing their way up her stomach. She felt the curves that led to her breasts and allowed her fingertips to linger at the place just beneath the rise. She traced the spot with her index fingers, surprised at how soft and sensitive it was. She left her right finger there, and allowed her left hand to drift up, over her breast. Her fingers encircled her nipple and gave it a tug. She arched her back in response and pinched it harder, tugging it again, gently. A moan slipped from between her lips. Z repeated the motion again and again, pinching, then pulling. Pinching, then pulling. Her left hand drifted from the pit of her shoulder to the swell of her hip. She slowly rubbed the side of her hip, reached around, and squeezed the flesh of her backside before sliding her hand back up.

She felt her skin get hotter and hotter, her hips instinctively rocked in circles as she kept up the motion of her hands. She lost track of her moans and felt a soothing sense of peace begin to envelop her. Z wanted more. She was just about to reach down, dip her fingers into the forest between her legs, when the phone rang and startled her to attention. It rang again and she stumbled up to answer it, modestly pulling her nightdress down over her knees and looking around to make sure she was alone.

Yes? Hello, Auntie—Yes, I will finish the laundry and wash the morning dishes—The chicken from the freezer? OK, I'll take it out right now—OK—Yes, Auntie. I know I stayed out late, but—OK. OK, Auntie—Yes. Yes, I know. I'll talk to you when you get home. Yes—Good-bye—

T hung up before she could finish. Z puttered around the kitchen for a while, stacking the dishes and getting the drainer out to set them to dry. She pulled the chicken out of the freezer and placed it in water to defrost. When the water poured over her fingers she almost jumped. Her skin was still burning.

Giving up on the concentration needed to clean, she tried to sit and watch television. Curling up on the sofa Z grabbed the remote and turned on the set, flipping from channel to channel to channel. As the images went by in a blur she thought back to when she was little, when she would lie still and quiet, touching herself until she shook. She remembered the innocent joy, and tried to imagine a richer, fuller, grown-woman gratification.

She cursed her body, cursed her curiosity. She sat up straight and wondered aloud if she was supposed to feel pride in the scar she was left with, or the self-hate coursing through her veins. She questioned what she was doing at all here in this cold, lonely city, speeding toward winter. Maybe she should have just stayed home and gotten married to her intended, followed expectations. Why had she been so headstrong about coming to America and going to school, about trying to find some big, exciting life? Maybe she had fooled herself into loneliness and pain and starless skies.

Z found herself lying across her bed with her face pressed into the pillow. She felt the cotton case soak up her hot tears and spread them cool across her cheeks. Her body was almost feverish. Slowly she let her hands lift her nightgown up and over her head. She buried her face back into the wet pillow as her fingers trailed almost imperceptibly up her thighs. She let them linger, drawing circles with one hand, while the other reached up to cup her breast.

Sweat dripped like dark rum down her temples, riding the salty rails of her tears. It broke out like dew along her arms and chest. With one hand pinching and pulling her nipple, she let the other drift impatiently between her thighs. She settled her fingers along the scar she had cursed so many times, and for the first time she felt how soft it was. The skin was damp and getting slicker. She spread the wetness around and felt herself getting warmer still as she circled her fingers around the spot. She moved her hand around and rubbed the space where her thighs met her small opening, front to back. She rubbed slowly, then more quickly, returning to the scar with which she was slowly, seductively becoming enamored. Each rough edge swelled to caress her fingertips, like lips welcoming her into a kiss.

The palm of her hand was pressing into bone where her thick, black curls began. Her breath started coming hard and fast as she rubbed her forearm across one breast and gripped the other's nipple tight between her fingers. Pinching and pulling. Pushing and circling. She became enraptured by the rhythm as her body danced. She felt as though she'd never heard music before, never felt the freedom of movement.

At first, it almost felt like laughing. Her shoulders started to softly shake. Her lip trembled. She felt a squeezing, like a firm, desperate handshake gripping the pinky she pushed inside. Her fingers grasped their nipple more tightly. Teeth clenched. A grin would have pulled her lips apart and spread like sunshine across her face if her mouth hadn't been so busy birthing a scream. If her throat hadn't already been choking up moans of *never befores* and the blessings of honey-coated wholeness she found deep inside herself, then, yes, she would have been laughing. Throwing her head back and laughing at the astonishing simplicity of it.

Falling back on the pillows as she gasped for breath, Z ran milky fingers up her stomach, dragged them across her chest. They lingered on her neck, glided up her cheeks and over her lips. When they found their way into her mouth, her tongue lovingly bathed them, savoring the nectar as its flower twitched her continuing release.

Z woke up and realized she had less than two hours until her cousins returned from school, and T would be home soon after. She balled all the dirty clothes she could find into her sheets, threw the nightgown on top, and headed downstairs to the washer. The rest of the afternoon she was astonished by the brilliant light that filtered in through the kitchen blinds. The sudsy water felt like warm ocean waves caressing her skin. The reds and oranges in the living room draperies had never looked so bold. The blue shag of the carpet held a brilliance that she was amazed she hadn't noticed.

At dinner, everyone complimented her on how rich her chicken and rice tasted. Even though she made the same dish every Thursday night, she couldn't help but agree that tonight it was especially flavorful. Every spice exploded across her tongue; each drop of sauce seemed to make love to her lips before it mixed perfectly with the rice and slid down her throat.

Z walked to work that night with an extra swing in her step. Her hips swayed and her backside bounced as she reached her fingers out to the leaves hanging heavy over the brownstone fences. It was another moonless night, and Z studied the sky as she made her way around the park. She took her time counting the stars, careful not to miss any. She was stunned into silence by the starry night overhead. In the distance she could see the Archer, the constellation her mother dedicated to her before she left home. She felt her mother's arms around her, understanding.

As Z rounded the corner into the hospital parking lot, she felt closer to home than she had in years. She felt herself fully contained in the warm wrapping of her body. A small, secretive smile crept across her face as the automatic doors opened before her. Yes, she thought. She could get used to living here. This might be the perfect place to start the new life she had yet to imagine. Part of her hoped she could pick up an afternoon double shift so that she could share the news with Reagan. The other part of her couldn't wait to get back between her bedcovers. She was ready to start dreaming of the future; and she already knew the ideal way to lull herself to sleep.

Maddie's Journal
Camille Banks-Lee

On Friday morning, at 5:58 A.M., Rick rose just minutes
before the alarm clock rang, grabbed the remote, and
switched on ESPN for the early edition. "Booyah! Kobe and
Shaq strike again as the Kings suffer a devastating loss in the
fourth quarter." Disgusted, Rick turned off the television
and began his morning regimen of 500 crunches and 100
push-ups. Going out for a run used to be the high point of
his day. Exercise had become the biggest stress reliever in the
Shelton household, until the injury that forced him back to the
proverbial bench.

Rick was a weekend warrior who played organized
basketball and football any chance he could get. His thin
frame could no longer provide him the cushion he experienced
after eating a whole pizza when he was just twenty. He still
looked good in clothes but the Krispy Kremes had certainly
caught up with his six-pack. Rick was the bursar at the
University of Rhode Island, and financially he and his wife
were debt free and always in the black. This fact made Rick
happier than any other. But, nursing a torn ACL, he was stuck

in the house forced to watch daytime television and find other outlets for his boredom.

He grabbed his crutches and hobbled into the bathroom. With his wife away, Rick had another week to wait until his next marital copulation, and was left with chicken-choking as his only form of sexual release. Remembering that all of his audiovisual aids were locked in his office at work, and feeling the chubby in his briefs, he looked in the video tower for something that would take him to the next level. Finding nothing with a rating higher than PG-13 he grabbed his only option, the wedding video.

Maddie had told him she found it embarrassing, but he could not get over how comfortable and enticing she appeared in the video. His bride was completely naked in it for the first twenty minutes as she was indulged and bathed by her bridesmaids. Renee, Maddie's sister-in-law, had felt creative and decided to do a takeoff on the opening scene of *Coming to America* where Eddie Murphy is being prepared for marriage. The gentle spraying of rose water on her face awakens her. In a white T-shirt and thong Maddie appears more like Chaka Khan than her usual Lois Lane. Her hair is bushy and wild. Renee pulls off her clingy T-shirt and uses sweet almond oil to moisturize her entire chest. Maddie's dark areolas are smaller and less protruding than they are now, but the shots of just the fingers on the nipples and the varied shades of hands loving them made Rick long for a piece of the action. As the oil puddles onto the small of her back, the manicured fingers seem to disappear into her fleshy thighs. Her back is arched as the camera focuses in on her clearly enjoying both the attention and the massage. There appear to be a few breaks in the action, but by the time Maddie is in the bathtub, there is a pretty good mess on the sheets.

After successfully fulfilling himself Rick fell into a deep

slumber only to be startled by the annoying ring of the phone on his nightstand.

"Hello?"

"This is MasterCard, can we please speak with Madison Shelton?"

Always handling the financial affairs of the family, Rick sharply stated, "Yes, go ahead, please."

"Well, Mr. Shelton, the charges on your card exceed the normal daily balance and as a safety check, we are just inquiring about the recent purchases in Providence."

"What?"

"Sir, there are numerous recent charges on your bill, from the Motel 6 in Providence and the Kitty Cat Lounge, which we just need to verify so that we can prevent fraudulent activity."

"Yeah, well, that has got to be some kind of error. I haven't been to a Motel 6 in, like, ten years."

"According to our records you have been there at least three times since June 2001. Mr. Shelton, before we begin the preliminary phase of our fraudulent spending investigation, we need to ask you a few questions. Of the two cards registered with this phone contact, is it possible your domestic partner, or uh, significant other, Richard Shelton, is responsible for these charges unbeknownst to you?"

"First of all, my wife, Madison, does have a separate MasterCard, but I can assure you that she ain't at no Motel 6 either."

"Sir, I specifically asked to speak to Madison Shelton. I can no longer speak to you about this account since it is registered to a name other than yours. Please ask Mrs. Shelton to notify us, at 1-800-555-4444, at her earliest convenience." Click.

Rick could not believe she hung up after dropping some news like that. What the fuck was going on? On *Oprah*, just yesterday, Dr. Phil said that it was crucial for couples to maintain a strong level of intimacy and that secrets were not appropriate in any circumstance. He was sick of being shut out of Maddie's life. Today he would find out the answers to many of the mysteries that intrigued him about his wife. Of course, he would pay for this betrayal somehow, but he convinced himself that what he was doing was taking a bold step toward saving his marriage.

He realized that what he wanted to know about her could only be found in her locked shrine of memories. To her, it was the most exquisite piece of furniture they owned. It was solid mahogany with a huge silver *ohm* as its latch. It came from the Ming Dynasty and was given to her by her university's history department. The journals that she kept inside served as Maddie's memories, a part of her soul and a way for her to know herself in ways she could never share. Fumbling through the kitchen for a suitable weapon of choice, he found a metal nail file in the junk drawer and hoped it would be as easy as *Rockford* made it look.

Thumbing the lock Rick took the nail file and gently moved it along the grooves of the opening. The lemon oil she used to clean and shine the piece made it slick to the touch. He was surprised to look down and see that his white BVDs were sticking to the couch from his sweat. He was even more amazed when the lock popped and he saw what lay inside.

"Damn," Rick muttered to himself as he lay dazed and confused on the couch amidst a pile of books. Looking at the journals, he shook his head silently. Rick had no idea there were so many of them. There were at least thirty in all different shapes, sizes, and colors. Some of the covers had juvenile themes like teddy bears, hearts, and unicorns. When he spotted the one of brown hand-sewn leather with the turquoise dream-catcher and the silver latch, he knew he had struck gold.

Rick was not much of a reader, but he was proud that both

his wife and his daughter considered reading a hobby and collected books like stamps. He didn't know where to start as he looked through the pile. He picked up the soft leather journal and his fingertips felt warm as he leafed through the gold-edged pages. The thing that he noticed first was all the tickets and receipts that had been glued to the pages. The first entry that he stopped at had a folded receipt from the Motel 6 on Route 280. It was placed in front of her handwriting:

I took my bra off in the car and hoped that my dark areolas would not poke through my white bodysuit. My pussy was aching before I even saw him. Tonight began with just me and Reggie dancing close, smoking weed and drinking tequilas at the gay bar out by Provincetown. The music was seductive and the smell of his sandalwood oil was intoxicating. He was rubbing himself against me and playing with my hair as we listened to Sade sing. I rested my head into his neck and began nuzzling up to him. I sucked on his middle finger and played with his wedding ring in my mouth. His fingers seemed to match the thickness of his dick. I loved having them in my mouth almost as much as I loved tasting the sweet heaviness of his balls.

Hearing noises upstairs Rick closed the journal and sat straight up. For the past ten years of their lives together, Rick had watched his wife conduct a nightly ritual of writing in her journal. There would be times that she would come in late and not even kiss Allison goodnight or brush her teeth but she would always manage to get to that damn shrine and start writing in her book. When he encouraged her to make some money with those "stories," she would only smugly say that she was not a writer. She had to be the most writing nonwriter in history.

Madison worked as an associate librarian at Brown

University. She loved books and she loved people immersed in research. She was also a control freak who loved order and accuracy. Madison seemed to have few passions, but one of them certainly was reading and writing. At home, Maddie became the Ice Queen soon after the wedding. There was sex on Sundays before breakfast, but that was only with her on top. On special occasions, like their anniversary, there was oral gratification. For a woman who seemed to enjoy sex as much as she did, he thought it was a shame she did not let herself go more often. For the most part Rick was happy with their perfunctory arrangement. He was more than happy with a beautiful wife and daughter, the mortgage being paid in advance, the house routine being tight.

Maddie got off on dressing in the porno-librarian chic that was seen in X-rated films. Her uniform consisted mostly of blue or black pantsuits, worn with a rainbow of Lycra bodysuits that barely held her crowded bosom. In fact it was the only thing that appeared to be deliberately sexual about her. She liked to be looked at but only on *her* terms. Her full body was ripe with fleshy thighs and pendulant breasts. Her cleavage was as natural a part of her body as the deep dimples that always appeared when she smiled. The eyeglasses she wore were petite tortoiseshell ovals that masked nothing. Her skin was smooth like peanut butter, marred only by the small freckles on the bridge of her nose. On most days she wore her hair in a stern brunette bun. The only time it hung loose was when she played seductress.

In her world, she likened herself to a modern-day Mata Hari, or at least one of Charlie's Angels. Her job as a librarian kept her safe from speculation about the reality of her dual lives. It was the perfect cover and it allowed her the freedom to live life on terms she constructed. Her other life made being a wife and mother tolerable.

The grandfather clock in the dining room alerted Rick

that Allison would be awake any minute. Before he even had a chance to gather up all the journals from the floor, he looked up to see his daughter's smile. She knew at once there was something wrong. Allison was determined to avoid her father's eyes. She wanted to retreat and go back upstairs with Nancy Drew, but it was too late, she had been spotted. Rick hoped that she could not see over the breakfast nook and into the living room. Before he had a chance to come up with a lie, she quickly blurted, "So, Daddy, are we still going out to see Uncle Jimmy?"

"Uh, yeah," Rick stammered. "Of course. Get yourself ready after breakfast."

Just like her mother, this girl was a master of the routine. At the same time every day, she went into the kitchen for her bowl of Cheerios. She would get a book and sit and eat and read. Allison was nine, precocious and independent. Her parents needed her, as the only child, to take care of herself, and she did. They had her conditioned to need very little, and she liked to pretend to be invisible.

He could not resist the temptation of reading more so he grabbed the dream-catcher journal and read on:

Renee was acting funky today saying she is not sure if she will be able to make it out tomorrow night. This may be my only chance to get out this month. It's not like I need her to be there in order to really get my freak on. Shit, the minute my lips wrap around that fat dick I am in heaven. When I first brought her in she needed a couple of drinks to get her going, but that was when it was just me and Reggie. God, we were so in love with the freedom of what we were doing. His black ass is such a show-off. It's hard to believe we have been fucking all these years. I have not gotten bored with her yet, but she can be very lazy when it comes to eating my pussy....

Rick was startled by his daughter's shrieking voice. "Daddy," Allison screamed from the top of the white staircase, "did you wash my yellow bathing suit?" Rick laid the journal on the center of his chest and rubbed his temples. Reaching into his night table drawer he took out a stale pack of Newports and a lighter. At that moment he was not sure how he had ever actually quit.

"Look in the wicker hamper in the hallway," he yelled back. At that moment, he needed to smoke that cigarette more than he needed to continue reading, but there was no turning back.

"DAD, I don't see it, can you come help me get the summer stuff out of the attic?"

Stepping over the mess, with the journal still in hand, Rick got up and walked to the mount of the staircase. The phone rang and broke the stillness of the living room.

"Don't answer that!"

"Why!!!!!!!!!, I can see from the caller ID it's Uncle Jimmy!" Maddie's younger brother Jim lived an hour and a half east of Providence in Hyannis and hated it. He was always looking for company because he had not yet made many friends. After his divorce from Renee, he managed to get custody of his three kids every single weekend. Whenever Rick was left alone with Allison for the weekend, he postponed his games and they met up for miniature golf, bowling, ice cream, and so on.

Picking up the receiver in the front hallway, Rick balanced the phone on his chin while trying to find his place back in the journal. "Hey Jimmy, I am just getting Allison's bathing suit and shit together. We should be out there by noon."

"Cool, I was just confirming because when I picked up the kids last night Renee wasn't sure if Maddie was still going to that research conference in New Haven." Jimmy chuckled, "I think Renee is in need of that sister-girl bonding shit, ya know. That damn book club won't meet for another month and she always acts better after that little bullshit."

Allison clicked on from the upstairs phone, "Uncle Jimmy, are you on the way to meet us?"

"Yeah, baby, I will see you guys soon!"

"Hold up, Jimmy, let me ask you a question. Allison, hang up the phone and get your butt in the shower!" After he heard the click of the extension, Rick lowered his voice and asked, "Do you keep a journal like your sister?"

"Whoa, whoa, dead that, the only vicious fight we ever got into growing up was about that damn journal of hers, I stole that shit once and when she found out she threw an iron at me, you see that scar on my left cheek?"

"Yeah, yeah, uuhhh, whatever, cool. Is it all right if Allison spends the night with you tonight and I will pick her up tomorrow? I am not sure, but I may need to do some work tonight."

"Shit yeah, I hope the 'work' you have to do is worth it!"

"Alright man, I'll let you know when I am on my way there. If anything comes up, just hit me on the cell." Rick closed the door to his private bathroom and reached for the wedding picture that was set upon the bureau. He was looking for visible signs of clandestine behavior in her face. Lying on his stomach with his feet on the pillows, he grabbed the journal and began to thumb through all the pages with receipts attached. Many of them appeared to come from that same motel on Route 280. The first page read:

I missed him the minute he got out of the car. I love the trepidation and intense passion that is between us. I stare at the ceiling and think of tomorrow night's events and I am finally able to make myself wet enough for him to enter me. I can't bear another night with Rick. I love the action between the four of us, but I would like to bring another girl into the festivities with us. Reggie loved having me to himself, but my appetite has grown to the point where one man and one woman is hardly enough of a feast for me. I hate that I always have to be the closing act because after Renee comes, she is of no use to anyone. She is my heart, but after she comes like a banshee she just lays her fat ass across the bed as if she were the Queen of Sheba. That dumb-ass brother of mine had no idea of what to do with that ass! Ha!

On another page was a hastily written note:

I miss you already and that's what makes this so hard. I am so hard and thinking about kissing you and you're pulling away. You have walked so long with one foot out the door. Please don't shut me out; I need you so much more than he does. Each time I drink you in with thirsty eyes and kiss you, your lips taste like hope, like love. The last time we were together I hated having to share you with so many. Don't you remember the fun we had when it was just us? Why am I not enough for you anymore? Even when it was me, you and Renee, it was better than the circus we have now....

The note was ripped so that he could not read the rest of what had been written.

"Daddy!" Before he could reply, she burst in shouting, "Are you dressed yet?"

"Allison, you know better!"

He was caught reading his wife's journal and he knew that his daughter had seen the book. As much as they had discussed privacy as a family value, it could not be any more hypocritical than to bust her for opening the door as he was sitting there reading his wife's secrets. "Close that door and put your stuff in the car, I am almost ready."

"OK!"

Rick thought of stories he could make up that would

conceal this act. He knew that Ali would be confused if she knew what he had done. "Ali, honey, I need you to be on your best behavior tonight. I am not going to be there. There is somewhere I need to go, alone. I will pick you up in the morning."

"Great, you are acting kinda weird anyway."

Once in the car Rick succumbed to Allison's many pleas to hear the new Britney Spears CD on the entire car ride up to Jim's. He needed the time to zone out and think about what he was going to do if he caught his wife with another man. It was not an image he was prepared to deal with.

Arriving at the diner Jim smacked his brother-in-law on the back and gave him a mischievous wink as he left with Allison. Rick did not feel comfortable sharing anything with him because he was still not sure of how he was going to proceed. The bad thing was that he was turned on by the whole scene more than he was turned off by it. His dick was throbbing at the idea that his wife was having so much sex. He felt delirious. Maybe this was a big fantasy for her and she was scared to share it with him? Didn't Oprah say that many women use journals as an expression of the life they wanted to live, but not the actual life itself? He was determined to find out that night which was actually true. Oddly, he felt more alive at that moment than he had in years. He was on a mission, like James Bond in *Octopussy*, and felt more intrigued than angry so far.

In the hotel parking lot Renee's VW Beetle and Maddie's Subaru were parked next to the Coke machine and ice dispenser. Rick took out the binoculars he brought and adjusted them to peek directly into the room in front of their parked cars. The shadows he saw clearly outlined the feminine forms of two women, and possibly a third. The woman standing appeared to be speaking in an animated manner, but it wasn't clear if it was his wife or Renee. Swallowing hard,

Rick searched the car for soda pop money. He had no other choice but to go out and get to the bottom of this mess.

Finding success in the crevices of the car seats, he walked over to the neon red light, bought a Coke, and looked directly into the only room lit before him. There was an eerie indigo glow coming from the room, which Rick assumed to be candles. Standing dangerously close to the window, Rick peered in and saw his wife in an unfamiliar red lace bra and panty set with a huge, empty wine glass on the table in front of her. She was pecking away at her laptop and taking pauses to read aloud.

Renee stood over Maddie with a red pen in her silky pink mouth and a stack of papers in her hand, rubbing Maddie's shoulders. Renee's pink satin bathrobe was crushed against her dark skin, and the heaviness of her naked breasts prevented the robe from fully closing. The contrast was startling. Damn, Rick thought, he did not remember Renee being so damn fine.

Maddie turned away from the computer abruptly and grabbed the papers out of Renee's hands. She stood up and pulled Renee close for a hungry kiss. Maddie reached out and released one of Renee's breasts from the pink robe and caressed it gently with her tongue. She engulfed one whole titty and steadily massaged the other through the robe. Renee helped her by untying the robe and pressing her body against Maddie's. Maddie grabbed a chunkful of ass with both hands. They sucked lips and licked each other's necks until Renee tore herself away. She came back with a male blow-up doll.

"Meet Mimbo. I got him at the Kitty Cat." Rick pressed his ear to the glass, hoping the girls wouldn't see him.

"Shit," said Maddie, "his ass is about as heavy as Rick's!"

"Let's let him watch us," Renee giggled and propped Mimbo up in a nearby chair. Maddie sat on the side of the bed sipping another glass of Merlot. Leaning toward her with teasing eyes, Renee got on her knees and whispered up Maddie's inner thighs. Her locks fell across Maddie's lap and she buried herself in her sweet, red-lace-draped pussy. Renee yanked the panties aside and plunged fully into Maddie's nectar. She alternately circled, teased, and sucked her clit hard.

They appeared, to Rick, to know each other's needs quite well. As Rick watched through the window, Renee lifted Maddie off the edge of the bed so that she could rub her juices into her ass and feel the fullness of Maddie's body grinding into her face. They moved in a rhythm that Rick had never seen. Renee seemed intoxicated as she held onto Maddie's hips and waited for her moans of approval. Maddie's closed eyes, pursed lips, and gentle shudder closed the deal.

"Damn," Maddie said, after her release. "I wanted to use him on the first round!"

Straddling the chair with Mimbo, Renee eased herself down on him inch by inch, pumping deliberately and controlling the movements. Within seconds, she began to buck wildly on the twelve-inch plastic cock, feeling the ripples of its well-constructed anatomy with each thrust. As she lifted her ass in the air, she kissed him playfully. Looking rejected, Maddie climbed behind her and mashed her tits against Renee, crying, "Don't forget me!"

"Take off that damn bra," Renee replied breathlessly, "and let me feel them titties on me. Yeah, like that."

"Like that?"

"Oooh, put your finger...yeah, girl.... Damn, I needed this. His dick is better than any I ever had. Too bad I can't get no response out of his fake ass!" Her legs wrapped around Mimbo's body, Renee came in long, shattering spasms before both women rolled to the floor and out of Rick's sight.

Rick drank in the lush luck of the moment. Still stunned, he felt armed with an odd sense of relief as he rubbed the cold soda can over his forehead, breathed deeply, and walked back to his car. With his dick in his lap, and no more answers about his wife than he had hours earlier, he moved rhythmically to the beat of the scene that both began and ended his day. He thought, as he stroked his way to release, that his 007 mission was just beginning. He loved what he was learning about his quiet wife. He couldn't wait to dig even deeper for more.

Lujon 1
Kimberley White

"Welcome home, Madison." The feminine voice of my household computer greeted me upon body scan recognition.

I stepped inside, still not used to hearing the overly chipper voice that grated on my last nerves. I was a member of the domicile government—didn't I deserve to have more than standard issue on government-funded housing?

I plopped down in the center of my *U*-shaped sofa. "Warmer," I groused at the household computer system.

"Warming to seventy degrees." She tried to please me as the walls swelled and radiated heat into the room.

Nothing would. I missed Rosie. Rosie was more than a robotic household accessory. Rosie kept me company on lonely nights and made sure I was well fed. I had saved for years to purchase her. A week ago she conked out on me and I couldn't afford the repairs. The manufacturer promised to make restitution—me being a member of the domicile government and all.

Meaning well, when my parents were approached by the Physician Administrator and asked to select my sex and occupation at six months' gestation, they condemned me to a life of boredom and seclusion as a female domicile official. Holding office on the middle tier of the domicile government, I lived decently inside the colony but had little power. Working in a noble profession, sitting on the governing body of our colony, I earned only modest wages. The destruction of the ozone layer in 2075 eliminated life outside the pods in most of the United States of America but didn't alter the need for currency.

It was now unsafe to venture outside the tempered walls without the proper gear. Scientists quickly developed colonies, including everything one would need to live one's entire life without going outside. Solar energy reproduced day and night; the weather was always sunny—what historians called "summer."

Unable to stand my household computer's chirping anymore, I woke early Monday morning and made my way to Robot Depot. I waited at the rail station with a few stragglers. Most were at church or relaxing this early on Resting Day. The railcar came and we few boarded. The rail crossed the expanse of the colony in very little time. The vast expanse of the historic state of Texas, Colony 629, was an intricate network of homes, businesses, hospitals, and schools.

On days when I questioned the meaning of my twenty-seven years in the colony, I wondered what it had been like to live outside it. Television brought images of what the United States used to be. Textbooks filled in the missing pieces. Old-timers spread unsubstantiated rumors that there were a few humans and animals living without pods in Alaska.

The railcar stopped a few doors down from Robot Depot.

"Welcome to the Robot Depot. Would you care for refreshments?" A pleasant-looking woman greeted me at the entrance.

I plucked a bagel off her tray.

"Whom are you here to see, Madison?"

I stared in wonderment. The fact that the woman knew my name meant she had used her eye scanners to perform a body scan on me.

"Amazing." I couldn't believe the realism of this robot.

"I am sorry. There is no one here by that name."

I stopped staring and remembered why I was at the Robot Depot on my day off. "I'm here to see Walter Ward."

"This way, please."

I followed the robot into Mr. Ward's office.

"Madison, have a seat." Mr. Ward greeted me and dismissed the robot.

My parents had taken me to visit the colony zoo when I was a child. Mr. Ward reminded me now of the cloned walrus.

Mr. Ward and I haggled over the terms for Rosie's repair. On my salary, I couldn't afford to have her fixed. Because she was a late model, most of the repair parts were costly to manufacture.

Mr. Ward reared back into his chair. "I want to do right by you, Madison. My daughter will be coming to the domicile government when she turns eighteen—I'd like to know she has a friend there." He popped upright in his chair and I thought he might propel himself over the desktop. "I'll tell you what I'll do. Robot Depot has developed a new version of the household robot that we plan to release later this year. If you're willing, I can give you a model to test for us. It'll be yours to keep, of course. You'd get a new, state-of-the-art, never-been-released robot. Robot Depot would get a consumer tester—at no cost to either of us."

I thought about my answer for less than a second. "Yes. I can live with that." I would be the envy of all my neighbors. I'd have the latest robot model before others could order it from the catalog.

The next Monday, my new robot was delivered. The technicians from Robot Depot opened the tall crate and revealed Lujon 1. Even though I had custom ordered my new robot, I was amazed at how closely he resembled the image of my perfect man: tall, with lustrous bronze skin, perfect white teeth, solid thighs, and strong-looking arms with a network of "veins" running beneath. Lujon's eyes were icy gray with no signs of the circuitry behind them. My body responded as violently as if Lujon were a flesh and blood male.

Lujon stepped out of the crate with a look of bewilderment that quickly disappeared when his eyes fell on me. As if he instantly knew what he was there to do.

"Wow."

One of the technicians laughed. "Can't tell the difference between him and a real man."

"No, I can't."

The technician waved me around behind Lujon. He lifted one of the dark curls at the nape of his thick neck. "Here's your panic button."

I had to get in close and gaze deeply before I could find the button that would shut Lujon off in case of an emergency.

"Give us a call if you need anything. His accessories are in the kitchen next to the recharge unit." The technicians lifted the crate on the dolly and started for the door.

I ran after them. "Where's the owner's manual? How do I program him?"

"The Lujon comes preprogrammed. Just talk to him like you would any employee, any man."

The men made a hasty retreat, leaving me alone with the lifelike Lujon.

I approached slowly, walking in a full circle around his impeccable body.

"I'm Madison. I guess I should show you around and tell you what I expect."

"I'm Lujon." The depth of his voice made my legs buckle. "And I already know what you want, Madison."

The suggestive tone of his answer and the wicked grin crossing his lips made me ask what he meant.

"Lujon is the latest model of Robot Depot–produced robots—"

"Lujon, stop. Move past the programmed spiel. How do *you* know what I want?"

"I'm customized to meet all your needs."

I heard it again.

I'm? Robots didn't have the cognition to combine words into contractions.

Lujon continued. "While you customized me, Robot Depot scanned you. I have been programmed to meet all your desires."

"Desires?"

"Yes."

My eyes flashed something Lujon read and liked. His gleaming smile took me off guard. "Yes, I'm fully functional. I perform better than any human man."

"Perform?"

"I must be given permission by my owner before initiating that program."

Too anxious to see what this robot could do, I blurted, "Permission granted."

As Lujon approached I readied myself for a petal-soft kiss and a strong embrace. Lujon reached out and grabbed a fistful of my hair, yanking my head back. He stepped into me and pressed his lips—hard—against mine.

"Hey! What do you think you're doing?"

"Giving you what you desire." He whipped me around and prodded me toward the back of the house. "Where is the bedroom?"

"This isn't what I asked for."

"No, it's not. This is what you desire."

As I stumbled around the sharp curves of my home, leading Lujon to my bedroom, I understood what he meant. This truly was my fantasy. To be taken roughly by a gorgeous man who was utterly obsessed with pleasing me.

I let Lujon go to work. He tossed me onto the bed. I watched in awe as he jerked at his belt buckle, yanked at the zipper of his jeans, and tugged them down around his ankles. I scooted back on the bed, making him chase after me. Lujon lunged forward, capturing my ankles. He grinned devilishly, very happy with his speed as he stripped me of my slacks.

"Does it work?" I asked, staring at what looked like ten inches of steel protruding from a sandy-brown mound of wispy hair.

"Continuously," he smiled. "I will grow hard whenever I sense your presence."

Lujon jerked my ankles apart and climbed into my *V*. He grasped his penis and ran the tip down the glistening wet slit of my cunt. With a deep flex of his hips, he thrust into me. My back arched as he shoved every delicious inch of him inside me. Hard, long, and hot, he was better than any human man I had been with.

Lujon proceeded to fuck me. He pinned my wrists to the bed and taunted me with dirty words about how much I loved the sweetness of his painful pumping. I exploded before his lips touched my breasts. But he didn't care. He had no concept of stamina because he could go on to infinity.

Lujon remained inside me, and had enough control over his dick to make it flex inside me, fucking me from the inside out. I rocked my hips as he leaned over me, kneading my breasts. He licked the underside of each, palming them, massaging them. He took my nipple into his mouth, gently suckling me until I fell into the net of his false security. Just when my shouts became moans of pleasure, Lujon bit my nipple, sending a current of pain through me.

"Lujon—" I protested.

"Hush." He pulled his twitching dick from between my legs and dropped to the foot of the bed.

I readied myself to experience his eating me out. If it were anything similar to the painful pleasure he had just given me, I would gladly wilt and die.

Lujon pulled me down on the floor beside him. He directed me to lie on my back. He straddled my shoulders and flexed his throbbing penis in my face. This close up I could see the authenticity of veins and flesh. As if I had any doubt after the pummeling I had just received.

Lujon lifted his penis and tapped it against my lips. "Open up and live out your desires." He guided the swollen bulb of his penis between my lips. "Taste me. Taste you."

I lapped at the tip of his penis, waiting. He fed me more inches. More and still more until his cock reached the back of my throat.

My hands grasped his perfectly sculpted ass. His head fell back and he actually moaned as I went to work. He began a rhythmic rocking that progressed to a full-blown mouth fuck.

And then the most amazing thing happened.

Lujon shot his wad deep inside my mouth. He grabbed his penis and painted my tongue, chin, and jaws with his cum. I gulped it down.

"Your desire?" Lujon asked.

I licked my lips, savoring the mandarin orange flavor of his sperm. "My desire."

"What flavor would you like to try next, Madison?"

The calming bass of Lujon's voice washed over me. The hypnotic timbre had rocked me to sleep after our bout of vigorous sex. Slowly, I opened my eyes—afraid I would discover that the night before had only been a dream. The slats covering the windows of my pod were tilted to allow in thin strips of solar brightness.

Standing stark naked, his penis at attention, was Lujon 1. He smiled provocatively. "What flavor would you like to try next?" he asked again.

I pushed down my wild mane and slid up to the head of the bed. "What do you mean?"

"I am able to provide you with a variety of flavored cum."

"You can shoot a wad of whatever flavor I want?"

"Yes."

I ran my tongue over my teeth and tasted the remnants of mandarin oranges. My eyes roamed over Lujon's nude body. Flawless bronze skin, flat stomach, and thick thighs. My nipples hardened to rival his majestic steel rod. I glanced at the clock to see if I had time for one more go with my new robot.

"Is there a problem?" Lujon dropped beside me on the bed, his hand squeezing my thigh.

"I have to leave for work soon. But I'd rather stay with you and see what else your 'body' can do."

"Would you like me to call in sick for you? I would be happy to demonstrate my abilities."

I liked this robot more and more. Walter Ward had a hit on his hands.

"I *would* like you to call in for me, but I really need to go to work." I rustled my hair again. Then I remembered. Lujon was here to serve me. He didn't care if I had morning breath or if my hair was standing straight up on my head. He only cared if I had what I needed to be happy.

Lujon sprang from the bed, his dick bobbing up and down as a temptation. "I have prepared a hot bath. After I place you in the tub, I will prepare your breakfast." He scooped me up in his arms and carried me into the bathroom.

I weaved my arms around his neck and pressed my breasts

against his chest. He smelled of my perspiration, but when the aroma emanated from his body it smelled exotic and enticing. His dick teasingly pushed up into the place between my buttcheeks. I was fully aroused by the time Lujon lowered me into the tub and walked away. He had dimples centered above his ass—just as I liked.

Lujon had all the qualities I like in a man. Sensuous, but not a pushover. Firm, but not a bully. Attentive to my needs. A sexual predator, but one who only cared about making me climax.

Tall and handsome, Lujon also possessed every physical characteristic I found sexy in a man. Bright gray eyes that simmered with passion when he looked at me. A ten-inch penis that felt like a steel rod wrapped in lamb's wool and tasted of fruity flavors.

Sexy. The way his eyes seemed to peer into my soul as he casually slipped his fingers through his hair. I shivered as I sank deeper into the hot, sudsy water. Sexier than any man the government had granted permission for me to date.

"Madison?" Lujon stepped into the bathroom. Red underwear strained to conceal his erection. "It's close to the time you leave for work, and your breakfast is almost ready."

I closed my eyes and sank deeper, the bubbles brushing my chin. "Five more minutes," I crooned.

"You will be late." Lujon reached into the tub and lifted me out. The mark left by my perspiration had been replaced by the sweet aroma of cologne. I inhaled deeply. He had uncovered another of my weaknesses. If Lujon kept this up, I wouldn't make it to work today.

"What's that smell?" I buried my nose in the crook of his thick neck.

"Your favorite." No smile; just information that I should have known.

He carried me back into the bedroom and placed me on a

bedspread of fluffy towels. He covered my midsection with a blanket.

"Wow. This feels good. How did you get it so warm?"

"The oven." Lujon wiggled his thick eyebrows, sharing his secret. He lifted a towel and began to meticulously dry my feet.

"I don't quite understand your purpose," I remarked as his tender caress passed over the arch of my foot.

"Simple. *You* are my purpose. Your needs, desires, wants, safety. You are why I was created. I exist only to serve you."

I lifted my head to meet his gaze. Did he know that a naked gorgeous man standing at the foot of my bed, worshipping me with his body, mind, and soul—all circuitry—wasn't the norm for me? A simple, middle-level member of the domicile government, I hardly had any romantic experiences—those conveniences were reserved for the athletic and artsy types.

I clarified. "Do you mean that if I hadn't visited Robot Depot you wouldn't have been, well, manufactured?" It hurt to say the word. Lujon was more than a pile of metal and wires. "You wouldn't have been mass produced? Available in next season's catalog?"

"No." He continued to pat me dry, moving up my calf. "If I had not existed in your head, I would not be here today. When you outgrow me, cease to desire me, I will be destroyed."

"Fat chance that'll happen," I said as Lujon's huge hands moved up my thigh. I could feel the juices pooling at the apex of my triangle.

"I don't understand that expression—*fat chance.*"

"It means keep doing what you're doing and you'll never become obsolete."

If Lujon is the figment of my wildest imagination made real, no one would ever know he's a robot. I could ask permission from the government to date him. I could give him the command to act as my husband, sparing me the matchmaking process required for those without mates when Mandatory Matrimony went into effect on my thirtieth birthday. Every sexual fantasy that ever rattled around in my mind, Lujon would fulfill and not make me feel perverted. The possibilities were endless.

Lujon started at my feet—peeling the blanket back as he went—and applied heated coconut lotion to my skin. After massaging both legs and arms, he gave attention to my back. I quivered as he applied lotion to my belly and worked it into my skin in small, sensuously slow circles. When he finished oiling down my body, there was more cream pooled between my legs than on every inch of my skin combined.

He opened the blanket to cover my entire body. "Excuse me one moment."

I glanced at the clock before relaxing back against a mound of pillows. Going to work seemed a farther possibility.

Soon, Lujon placed a tray across my lap. I opened my eyes to scrambled eggs, ham, bacon, hash browns, toast, and golden pancakes. Also, a fresh fruit bowl, cheese cubes, and juice.

"Lujon," I said with a laugh, "what are you doing to me? Are you trying to have me admitted to the Self-Preservation Clinic?"

The domicile government, in its infinite wisdom, long ago penned a bill that made it mandatory for its citizens to be placed in a weight-loss residency program if they exceeded their ideal body weight.

Lujon tilted his head in confusion. "This does not please you?"

"Yes, but it's too much."

He watched me closely.

"Never mind. It's perfect." I cut into the stack of pancakes to illustrate my point.

His broad shoulders eased into a downward slope.

Lujon moved to the foot of the bed and did the most spectacular thing. He lifted my foot up to his mouth and wrapped his thick, dark lips around my big toe. He suckled, running his fingers up and down my calf, eyes closed, moaning. His tongue danced across each toe and the pad of my foot.

"Eat, Madison."

"*You* eat, Lujon."

Eager to obey, he lowered my foot and crawled between my legs. As tall and packed with muscles as Lujon was, he moved with the grace of a magical cougar. He bent my leg outward and began to trace tiny circles with his tongue on the back of my knee. The sensation shot through me like a stray bullet. I gripped the edges of the tray as his tongue moved upward to the pool of waiting cream.

"Release the tray." Lujon pried my fingers away and tossed the tray onto the floor with a broad swipe of his bulky arm. His fingers wrapped around my thighs, digging into the skin, as he pushed them apart.

"I'll have bruises by tonight," I reprimanded him.

"Those, and many more." He secured my hips and pulled me down in the bed before fixing his attention on my thighs again.

Lujon rested his head against my thigh, his cotton-soft hair starting a fire that exploded with the fierce heat of a grenade. His tongue leapt out, parting his lips. He lapped at the tight curls covering my triangle. I stiffened—electricity burned me with each flick. His tongue withdrew.

Lujon used his long fingers to part one—two—sets of my intimate lips. He exposed my clit, leaving me vulnerable. "Don't move," he ordered, his tone harsh and humorless.

I froze and waited to be dazzled by what Lujon would do next.

Because I *knew*. I knew I had a fantasy buried deep in the back of my mind. I wanted to see if he had found it. I had watched the dirty movies and gawked at the pictures in the nasty magazines. I wanted someone to eat my pussy with a frenzied expertise that would leave me breathless.

Lujon pulled the lips of my purring kitty farther apart. His fingers pushed forcefully against my pubic bone, bracing for leverage. He centered himself, torturing me by placing his lips a mere whisper away from my pulsating nub. A hot puff of air hit my clit. Ice chips rushed through my veins and I yelped from the fabulous sensations that erupted. With every lap of his tongue, my body rose from the mattress. My arms pushed against the headboard to keep me from flying away. His strokes were long and thorough, mimicking those made by a jungle cat.

"Lujon, pleeaazzz—" I begged for more.

Lujon's tongue tunneled deeper. He made tight circles around my dripping clit. Tiny electrical sparks skipped across my naked body. Without warning from my body to my mind, the spasms began. Tremors racked me as if I had been submerged in a tub of iced water.

"Damn." My fist hit the mattress.

Lujon's head popped up. "What is wrong, Madison?"

"I wasn't ready to come yet." I ran my fingers through his hair. "You were too good for it to end that fast."

Lujon gave me one of his devilish smiles. "I can make you come again. Do not be distressed."

"Lujon, humans can't perform without limitations the way a robot can."

"Madison, I know many things about a human woman's body. You can come again and again—as long as I am up to the task of making it happen."

Well, well, now.

Lujon adjusted his body so that he was lying flat on his stomach between my thighs. He hoisted my legs over his shoulders. His fingers dug deep, separating my folds for the greatest, easiest access.

Slow-slow, Lujon's tongue entered the tight tunnel of my pussy. Up-up, his tongue weaved deeper. He slithered past the slick walls, making sounds of joy all the way.

"Impossible," I muttered even as I felt the depths he could reach. "Im-pos-si-ble." With every syllable, Lujon's tongue widened until his tongue filled me as full as his cock had the night before.

His hands went to my waist and encouraged me to ride along.

"This-isn't-happening," I panted when I felt his tongue lick at my cervix.

Wider and wider, his tongue began to swell, filling my tunnel more and more tightly. Delicious pain. Unique pain that sizzled white-hot until it smoldered into a flash of ecstasy.

"Lujon," I cried out, still begging for more.

He didn't answer—his mouth was full.

I heard it before I felt it. *Rrrrr. Rrrrr.* The mechanical whizzing sound of a familiar kitchen appliance.

My body detonated with ripples of pleasure from the inside out. Lujon's tongue whirled inside me at the speed of a blender. In and out, spinning around in circles at top speed. In, out. Around and around and around.

I screamed with mind-shattering joy. My back arched off the bed. I thrashed to get away. And I pushed forward to get more. My thighs clamped down on Lujon's face, trapping him in the embrace of my desire. Pieces of my mind seemed to float away on the tide of my orgasm.

I dropped to the bed, panting hard. Perspiration dripped down the contours of my body. My hair stuck to my scalp. Lujon laid statue-still between my legs until the quakes controlling my body stopped. He didn't take his tongue away.

I closed my eyes and concentrated on breathing. I willed my heartbeat to slow down to a gallop. I focused on every nerve in my body. I feared Lujon had short-circuited me!

Tongue still inside my tunnel, Lujon moved the feather-light stroke of his fingers to my belly. His thumb grazed the top of my curled, perspiration-wet bush. His hands traveled up my body until he cupped my breasts. The width of his tongue shrank to normal. The length decreased until he had a tongue no different than a human man's.

"Lujon," I purred.

"Madison," he growled back.

His fingers continued to stroke my body. The sheets were soaking wet beneath me. The lotion he had meticulously rubbed into my skin had melted away. My breathing and heart rate were back to normal. I suddenly felt exhausted.

Lujon pinched my nipple.

"Ouch," I giggled, remembering the rough sex-play from the night before.

"You have had enough time to rest."

Lujon began with a subtle stroke that lulled me to the edge of sleep. When my breathing slowed, Lujon's tongue sped up. More aggressive strokes followed. He ventured into my tunnel and pulled out quickly. His fingers gripped my hips and thrust my body down on him. My exhaustion fell away and was replaced by sexual hunger.

Lujon's tongue curled upward. He hit my G-spot, and the uncontrollable tremors began again. I rocked my hips to Lujon's rhythm. My nipples grew so hard that pain etched a pathway through the flesh of my breasts. Instinctively, Lujon began a merciless massage of my nipples.

In no time I felt the slow burn of my third orgasm building in that special place between my belly and my pussy. My clit ached.

"Lujon, rub my clit."

Lujon never withdrew his tongue.

I swear it—he never pulled out.

But a second tongue curled out of his mouth and stroked my clit.

My head shot up.

Lujon tilted his head and flashed me a peek at the second appendage. In an instant, it disappeared. The split sensation remained. My tunnel—in, out. My clit—stroke, lick.

Then the explosion as the miniature tongue worked feverishly to please me.

Lujon tried to kill me last night.

I pushed the panic button located at the nape of his neck, underneath the clutch of dark, curly hair. With much effort, I pushed his weight off of me, licked the remnants of chocolate ice cream cum from my lips, and called Walter Ward.

"Don't worry," Walter assured me, "this is a minor glitch that can be fixed."

"How?"

"Our scientists are the best. The technicians will pick Lujon 1 up when you return from committee and we'll have him repaired in no time. We'll need you to come in to be scanned before the repairs are completed."

After the call, I sank into a hot bubble bath and relived every minute of the past month with Lujon.

Lujon had taken a conservative domicile official and exposed her—my!—fantasy world. The effects were devastating. I couldn't keep my mind on work. All I did was dream up more sexually daring exploits to try with my new robot. I went in search of raunchy toys. I watched soft-core and studied XXX movies, pointing out my interests to Lujon. By nightfall, I was the actress on the screen.

Lujon did other things, too, the things you'd expect a household robot to do. And he did them as efficiently as he fucked me. My apartment was spotless. If something broke, it was repaired within the hour. The cupboards and refrigeration unit were constantly filled. He lifted the heavy stuff. My checking account balanced to the penny. Breakfast, lunch, and dinner couldn't have tasted better if they'd been prepared by a gourmet chef.

Lujon was perfect.

But I was flawed. After all, it was my sexual fantasies that Lujon enacted. He was programmed to make my desires come true. It couldn't be his defect that all my desires were stuffed with sexual content.

I sank deeper in the tub. My body ached and burned. Bruises in the shape of Lujon's hand were darkening on my ass. Purple reminders pulsated where his fingertips clutched my breast.

These marks had come when I had tried to deny Lujon. After dinner, he had lifted me and carried me to the bed. A conversation at work made me shy away. Rumors had reached the domicile government that scientists had developed a series of robots that had sexual capabilities. The topic was added to the agenda for next week. The government needed to decide if this was illegal, unethical.

Not that having sex with robots was new to Colony 629. Two years ago the first MHC—Medical House of Copulation—was opened. This hospital-run facility provided robots specially equipped to serve both men and women. One must have a prescription written by a physician or psychiatrist to visit the facility. This was supposed to be a place to cure sexual dysfunction or to satisfy deviant behavior so that it wouldn't be inflicted on society. I've heard rumors of some of the government officials going there—without a prescription—to sample the offerings.

The reason the government chose to handle it this way was twofold. First, it could be taxed. And second, they wanted to keep the act of humans and robots fornicating medicinal and prevent any chance of emotional attachment. "What would happen," they argued, "if humans developed feelings for the robots? It's hard to separate sex and love. Our society would cease to exist." Like our prisons, no one speaks of the MHC in public. It is our colony's dirty little secret.

When I heard that having sex with Lujon might be illegal, I denied him. Told him I wasn't in the mood for sex. He simply tossed me to the bed and proceeded to convince me through our rough-and-tumble play. I told him to stop; he balled his fist in my hair and pushed my legs apart. I said I meant it; he bit my nipple. I tried to reason; he plunged his dick inside my pussy.

Somehow, the nipping and biting began to feel good. My mind told me to stop because I'm a member of the domicile government and should know better. My body said, *Shut the hell up and ride this dick like you'll never see another one again.*

Looking now at Lujon's deathly-still body spread across my bed made me feel guilty, because he only wanted to please me.

A month later, the domicile government returned a split decision on the next generation of robots. Protestors of the bill picketed outside our offices. Supporters countered with their own rally. Colony 629's president decided the issue would be tabled until next year—after all, no manufacturer had developed the technology at a price affordable to consumers as of yet. If only he knew.

If only he knew how much I missed Lujon since I sent him back to Walter Ward. My house was looking trashed. I didn't have time to clean and when I did, I was too tired. I ate all my meals at the cafeteria at work. My laundry went to the cleaners or sat piled on the washer.

Sunday night—the last day of the workweek—I dragged myself to the videophone to answer a week's worth of messages. My parents. Automated sales calls. An old friend wanting to catch up. Several hang-ups, undoubtedly from people protesting the latest debated bill.

Mindlessly, I let the messages play as I turned on the television. The entire in-wall screen lit up with a picture of the office building where I worked. I quickly switched the channels by chanting, "Next channel," until a vacation advertisement caught my attention. Soon enough my mind began to wander...Lujon and I lying next to the pool while he smoothed sunscreen on my back...Lujon and I in the hotel bouncing on the round, velvet-covered bed...Lujon dressed in formal attire pulling out my chair in a fancy restaurant...Lujon kissing me...Lujon caressing me...Lujon...Lujon...Lujon.

"Lujon...Lujon...Lujon—" I screamed as my body convulsed from my own touch, "Lujon!" And I knew I was in deep trouble.

The videophone tinkled and then, "Madison, you have an incoming call from Walter Ward."

I jumped up from the U-shaped sofa and sprinted across the room, narrowly clearing the ottoman. The face of the cloned walrus stared up at me.

"Madison, I've left you several messages—"

Damn. I hadn't played them all back.

Walter Ward continued, "Lujon has been reprogrammed. He's been ready for delivery for several days. Can we arrange a day and a time?"

My good sense commanded my mouth. "Mr. Ward, I'm a little concerned about having Lujon returned."

"My goodness, why?"

"With all the commotion surrounding the new bill governing robotic advancement—"

"What in the world does that have to do with Lujon 1?" He looked either genuinely puzzled or like the greatest actor ever genetically engineered.

I cleared my throat and let good sense lead me deeper into the fire—there would be no deniability if I persisted; after all, if I knew every detail, I couldn't fake ignorance. "Lujon can do certain things that the domicile government hasn't decided whether it's legal for him to do," I replied.

Walter Ward stuttered, stammered, looked incredulous, and then gave me an intelligible answer. "The Lujon series of robots is manufactured by the best scientists in the world, using the most advanced techniques available. This accounts for their realism. What the Lujon series of robots can and will do is determined by the mind scan of the owner."

"I understand."

He was covering himself. Placing the blame on the purchaser; condemning me for having a dirty mind. He had recruited a member of the domicile government—someone with as much to lose if exposed as he himself—to try the new generation of robots. I should have been angry. I thought of Lujon; I felt relieved.

I asked, "I completed your survey—"

"The engineers and scientists have reviewed your comments and complaints and have assured me the problems have been rectified."

I inhaled. Thought of my responsibilities as a member of the colony's government. I exhaled. Thought of Lujon. "Very good. Monday delivery would be appreciated."

"You want to replace me with a human man."

Lujon 1 emerged from the packing crate wearing well-fitting jeans and a tee that defined his six-pack.

I silently clutched the white card sent by Walter Ward. There was no sense in denying anything; Lujon had the privilege, by way of mind scan, of knowing my innermost thoughts.

"I do not want that," Lujon firmly stated. "While the scientists were repairing me, they left me standing in the corner of the room. For hours during the day and all through the night after they had gone home to their families, I stood alone in the corner. You talk to me as if I'm human." He paused. "I do not want to go back there again."

There was no condemnation in Lujon's tone; that came from inside me.

I opened my mouth to justify my actions, but Lujon walked away. I stared after him, trying to discern how he was different, when I noticed I was crumpling Walter Ward's note. I opened it: a generic thank-you note with the date of Lujon's next tune-up. At the bottom of the card were two silver coins that resembled the historic currency of quarters. Script writing beneath the first coin read, "Operational Manual." The second read, "Manufacturing Specifications." Beneath both, in Ward's handwriting: "Confidential information."

Lujon appeared without warning footsteps. "I ran a bath."

"Thank you." I glanced down at Lujon's crotch. It grew to life in front of my eyes. Some things, thank goodness, were the same.

Some things were different. Lujon walked away. Was he shunning me? Was he trying to express the human emotion of anger? I had missed him terribly. I wanted him to lift me and carry me to the bath. I wanted him to sit on the floor while I bathed and listen to me ramble. I wanted him to dry me, oil me, fuck me.

Before sinking into the tub, I placed the computer chips from Walter Ward in my visual chip player. I had closed the door, but chose to use the headphones anyway. I cued the operational manual first. Before my eyes, in midair, appeared Walter Ward. He rambled on with operational instructions about the Lujon robot series. I had spoken with him personally. I didn't need to view the chip. I cued the "Manufacturing Specifications" chip. I wondered with a throbbing head why Ward had sent it to me. I couldn't understand half of what the engineer explained. Just as I was about to turn it off, another man crystalized above my bath suds.

This scientist immediately won my attention when he spoke about the confidential material contained on the remainder of the chip being for authorized viewers only. The man went on to disclose the miracle behind the realism of the Lujon series. The "robots" were only one-half metal and wire. The other half of Lujon was made of flesh—cloned flesh.

"Madison?" Lujon's soft tap countered the bass of his voice.

I jumped, hitting the STOP button. In my haste, I dropped the visual chip player in the water. I hustled to retrieve it before it shorted out.

"Madison, are you all right?" Lujon asked, his tone concerned.

"Yes."

Lujon glided through the door as I retrieved the player. I opened the cylinder. The chips were melting.

"Damn!"

"Can I help?"

Sucking up the loss, I calmed down. "No, Lujon, everything is fine."

"I brought you a glass of wine." He pulled the long-stemmed glass from behind his back and with a dip and flourish he held it out for me.

"Thank you." I had thoroughly missed Lujon.

"Dinner will be ready very soon." He disappeared without plunging his huge hand into the water and fondling me as usual.

I gulped the wine and placed the glass on the edge of the tub. Lujon: half human. How did this muck up the laws we were arguing? Should Lujon be classified a well-trained human or an amazing robot? As much as I had enjoyed seeing the rise and fall of his ass as he walked away from me, I didn't care. This changed everything.

What parts are flesh and blood? His beautiful penis? No. He could not have inherited that work of art from any living being. Ten inches long, encased in wrinkled brown skin, topped with a bulbous head the width of a turnip, and shooting crystal-clear cum in a variety of flavors, no penis from any man could become so instantly and continuously erect and could so please me to tears.

And his ass.... His ass was definitely made of human tissue. Solid, high, and dimpled, it was surely human—I had squeezed it enough to know.

Abdomen? The six-pack was as hard as a steel plate, as soft as a pillow. I didn't know about the abdomen.

Thick, corded arms. Strong legs. Huge hands. Shimmering skin. Clairvoyant eyes. Infectious smile. Cotton-soft hair.

My head spun, trying to figure it all out.

I emerged from the bathroom dressed in a purple silk gown that grazed the top of my feet. I followed the delicious aroma of dinner into the kitchen, observing Lujon's work as I went. My apartment had been transformed into a middle-level showplace. The washer and dryer hummed in the distance. Candles burned in the living room, filling the apartment with a fragrance of cinnamon.

Lujon busied himself in the kitchen, never venturing far, while I ate dinner. I rattled on about my day and every event that had occurred while he was away. He folded clothes at the dryer, glancing over his shoulder from the laundry room. Always showing me I was the center of his attention.

"Would you like to watch television?" Lujon asked after clearing my plate.

"I would. Watch with me."

Lujon settled on the sofa, one leg outstretched along the back cushions. He swallowed my hand in his and tugged until I sat between his legs. His thick arms wrapped my waist. I let my head drop back against his chest. I had missed him so much.

"You seem different," I observed, "but I can't put my finger on what's changed."

"No?" His lips skipped across the top of my head.

A familiar warming started below my navel. "Do you know?"

"Do I know?"

"Yes. Do you know what repairs the scientists made?"

"None."

"None?" I craned my head around to face him. "They kept you an entire month. Is it possible they made repairs but you're not aware?"

"No."

"Then what were they doing to you all this time?"

"Changing me."

"Lujon," I said, exasperated. "Changing you how?"

"To meet your needs, desires, wants."

"You were programmed for that the first time."

"Madison," his voice dropped an octave, "your needs, desires, and wants have changed."

"Explain, please."

Lujon ran his finger across my jaw. His gray eyes captivated me. He gave me an Eskimo kiss before answering. "When I first arrived, you wanted a man to satisfy your sexual urges and live out your wildest fantasies. You now need someone to care for you. You desire a relationship that satisfies your soul. And you want a man to love you more than he loves himself."

Stunned, I gazed into Lujon's eyes. He dipped his head and stroked my temple. He captured my face between his hands and pressed our lips together. He tugged at my bottom lip until I opened to him. His tongue glided into my mouth and bathed me in magnificence. When he pulled away, I felt dazed and confused.

"Lujon," I breathed.

Lujon untangled our bodies and carried me into the bedroom. He moved around the room lighting candles and turning down the lights. When he finished, he stood at the foot of the bed and allowed me to watch him remove his clothes. His eyes never looked away. The corners of his mouth hardened with—what? desire?

I didn't wonder if or how he could feel emotions, only if the emotions were specifically for me.

"What are you thinking?" I asked as Lujon strolled to sit beside me on the bed.

"I don't want you to replace me with a human man." He splayed his fingers on my ankles and began to push my gown upward over my calves. "I can be all and more than any human man could be." My thighs. "Cook...." My hips. "Maid...." My belly button. "Master...." My breasts. "Child...." Shoulders.... "Lover." The gown went over my head and pooled on the floor.

"I will make love to you now, Madison." Lujon pushed my thighs apart and insinuated himself in the opening.

"I will prove to you I belong to you." He kissed my left breast.

"I will prove to you that you belong to me." Lujon kissed my right breast. He lingered, applying suction to my nipple that pulled it into his mouth. My body softened, moistened to the swirl of his tongue.

"I will prove to you I am more than metal and wires and circuits." His hand disappeared between us. I whimpered as he pushed and pushed until all ten inches of his glorious penis filled me.

"I will prove to you that I am your fantasy come to life." Lujon panted as he worked his hips. On a mission to make me submit, he pumped hard and fast, then as tenderly as the kisses he placed on my eyelids.

"Tell me," Lujon punctuated every thrust, "do I belong to you?"

My head fell back on the pillow. "Yes."

"Do you belong to me?" Thrusts, with a kiss to my temple.

"Yes."

Lujon made large, then small, circles with his hips. "Do you see me as more than metal and wires and circuits?"

"Yes!"

Lujon wrapped my legs around the indentation of his waist and drilled each word into my psyche by way of my intimate opening. "Cook. Maid. Child. Master—" he gathered my hair in his fist, but never lost the rhythm of his stroke. "Lover—" he buried the tip of his penis deep. I hung onto his hips to keep from skyrocketing to Saturn.

"Madison?" Lujon kissed my lips, my temples, as I rode the waves of ecstasy. "Can you love me as a man?"

"Could *you* love *me*, Lujon? Is it possible?"

"Haven't I proved, by my very existence, that all things are possible?" He nuzzled my perspiration-slicked breasts as he waited for my answer.

"Yes, you have."

"Madison, believe that I may not be one hundred percent human, but I love you." His thumbs brushed the arch of my brow. He pressed his forehead to mine and watched me with his smoldering gray eyes. No man—human or machine—could look at a woman in that way and not love her.

I threw away caution. "I believe you, Lujon."

"Do you believe you could ever love me as I love you?"

"I believe I already love you as much as you love me."

Lujon's lips found mine and he kissed me into our own private oblivion.

Crystal's Desire and Shango's Feast
Opal Palmer Adisa

Six months after Crystal's separation, her divorce pending, she was ready for a lover to take some of the edge off. Besides, celibacy did not improve her well-being; she knew she didn't lack self-love. What she needed was a man—no demands, just someone to satisfy her sexual appetite. Her only requirements were that he should be a good lover, disease-free, and discreet. Friends suggested the personal ads since she had been out of the dating game for more than fifteen years. After scanning a few, Crystal decided that was not the route for her, but she didn't know where to find the lover she craved. She definitely did not want an intellectual professional; she had had her full of that type. Crystal desired someone wild, adventurous, spontaneous. She had no particular look in mind, but was partial to someone who was toned, with a ready smile.

It was as if Shango walked right out of her fantasy—body solid, always a mischievous smile dancing on his face, and a thunderbolt in bed. He didn't care where they were, or who was around, he would pause and lick her neck in the middle of the sidewalk, put his hand under her skirt at the café where they sometimes had breakfast, unbutton her blouse and suck her breast in the parking garage, squeeze her behind and caress her thighs when they went walking. He was all over her, and she was always surprised that she never stopped him. In fact, she welcomed these public advances, their unrestricted sexual display. Yet she never took him to her home. Always, they went to his place, which was messy but homey, and there they made wild love that left her exhausted but with such a full feeling that for days after she hardly ate. Tonight was the first time they would make love at her house, and she hoped it didn't mean that she wanted him to be more than her lover.

Crystal's G-string panty rubbed against her vulva. She felt Shango's hands on her thighs, stroking them up, down, and around, and it took all her concentration to keep driving. Didn't he know what he was doing to her? She wanted to fling her legs wide and have him cool her heat, hose her down. She squirmed in the driver's seat. In less than ten minutes she was at her exit. Shango slid off his seat, was on his knees on the passenger side, and was close to tasting Crystal through her clothes. She slapped his hands away, playfully pushed his head from being caught between the steering wheel and her thighs, and told him to hang on, they would be home soon, and then he could ravish her. Once she exited the freeway, she slowed to the speed limit. Shango pouted.

Before the engine stopped rattling, Shango was out of the car and at the door. Safely inside her house, Crystal leaned against the door, breathing hard. Right there she pulled off the bicycle suit, cap, sneakers, and gloves and stuffed them into the canvas bag she had placed by the door for that purpose. She stood with her partially clad body pushed up against the door and used her right hand to caress her body, stroking her nipples, rubbing her hands over and between her thighs, fingering her clitoris through the lacy G-string, feeling her wetness.

She heard Shango calling, picked up the canvas bag, and
walked into the kitchen. She had never been able to persuade
Donald to do it on the kitchen counter. Shango wasn't
uptight at all. Crystal turned on the burner under the kettle,
climbed on the kitchen counter, and lay on her back. Shango
mounted her, sweeping jars of beans and pasta to the floor.
He smiled down at her, before licking her from head to toe,
not bothering to undress her. After he had sufficiently aroused
and teased her, he entered her like a cannon and their pleasure
bounced off the walls.

Crystal didn't want to rise, but the whistling of the kettle
was insistent. The kitchen was filled with the odor of sex.
Feeling deep satisfaction in her limbs, she rose slowly, slid her
legs over the edge of the kitchen counter, and jumped down.
She filled the teacup with boiling water, picked up a pot full
of ginger water that she had boiled earlier, and headed for
the bathroom. Shango was waiting for her there with a huge
grin on his face. She turned on the hot water faucet, poured
in the ginger water, added a handful of Epsom salts, some
frankincense crystals, and a dash of jasmine bubble bath. She
slowly lifted the crumpled camisole over her head, tossed it on
the floor, and tugged playfully at the G-string like a stripper
teasing voyeurs. Once it was below her bottom she slowly
raised her left leg and ever so slowly slipped her foot out of
the G-string, leaving it to dangle at her right ankle. Shango's
eyes grew big in his head. He knew she was a tease, with a
big appetite. A woman like that could be plenty of trouble:
the demanding, never-get-enough type. Crystal twirled the G-
string around her ankle then flicked it, her feet pointed, red
painted toenails shimmering.

"I will rub your back and then I'll have to leave," Shango
pleaded.

Crystal smiled, lit the red and white candles that she had
placed by the bathtub, and turned off the lights. Shango pulled

off his soiled clothes and stepped into the tub. The water was scalding. He reached for the cold water faucet to cool it down. Crystal sipped on her tea, watching him. *Just let him think he will get away with only washing my back,* she thought as she stepped into the tub and fitted her body perfectly between his open thighs. Instantly she felt his rod hardening against her bottom and she settled back comfortably against his chest.

Shango was not one to resist beauty. Crystal had come to him in great pain. She had been wronged, cheated. She wanted justice. He offered to help, even before she offered him a piece, and exhausted as he was he couldn't resist her. He blew on her neck and saw the small hairs on the back of her neck standing at attention. She pressed into him and wiggled her bottom against his shaft. He slid his wet finger into her mouth and she greedily sucked on it. With his free hand he lathered her garden, his middle finger found the way into her store-room, and his lips and tongue sucked the calcium knots from her shoulder blades and back. She was moaning softly, the flute of pleasure, moaning the deep bass, humming the melody, and chortling the guitar and drums combined—moaning the whole band, so that Shango was beside himself.

He took his other hand from her mouth and cupped her breast, the lather from the bath making her breast slide with ease up and down in his palm as he massaged, pressed, stroked, and squeezed. But he wanted to taste it in his mouth, drink her milk, nibble on her nipples, send her soaring. Reading his mind, Crystal turned and got onto her knees facing Shango with her great behind jutting upward, and she pulled Shango's mouth to hers. First she sucked on his lips, then nibbled at his tongue before sucking it into her mouth, until he felt as if she was going to swallow it from his mouth.

This woman is something else, he thought. Uncertain whether he dared to boast that no woman could outdo him, Shango was determined at least not to be undone by a mere human woman. The thought gnawed at his ego, so Shango rose up, grasped Crystal around her shoulders, and they rolled around in the bathtub, water spilling over the sides, soaking the mat and wetting the entire floor. Red bubbles swirled, sailing around the bathroom. They laughed, panted, steadied, then unsteadied, themselves. Lightning flashed through the window, and the tub trembled with thunder.

Crystal pushed Shango against the tile and brushed her lips against his faucet. Shango moaned thunder, his eyes flashed lightning. He rose above the clouds then returned to cool Crystal down. On all fours Shango entered Crystal, and kept pumping until her entire body trembled and a scream of agonizing ecstasy escaped her throat. Panting for breath, Shango thought, *Such decadent rapture*. He was surfeited. He tenderly brushed his lips against Crystal's, ran his finger over her nipples, and left her to a well-deserved sleep.

Sojourner's Truth
Ta'Shia Asanti

The foot-stomping twang of a distant blues guitar strummed through me as I entered the festival grounds. The sound and smell of barbecue sizzling nearby snaked its way up my nostrils. I stepped up to one of the dozen or so food vendors and ordered a grilled corn on the cob. I saturated it with margarine and chili powder and at the last minute decided to sprinkle it with just a dash of cayenne. I casually moved toward the bleachers, corn and ice chest in hand, where the rest of the music lovers were bobbing their heads and clapping their hands to the stank grooves and wicked rhythms coming from the stage.

Two steps from the entrance I spotted her. My ticket was still in my hand. I shoved it back down in my pocket as my eyes narrowed to take in the magnitude of her statuesque frame. She was absolutely stunning. Her tie-dyed, orange-gold, floor-length dress hugged every curve and fold of her voluptuous body. The cowrie shells that hung from the bottom of her dress shook like the shimmy in a Shekere. Coyly she sat, aiming her buttery thighs and watermelon breasts in my direction. She was slightly rocking, shielded by the shade of a father tree, her straw hat pulled down tight over bronze dreadlocks and cat-eyed sunglasses.

The reflection of her oval face and oak-colored skin made me simmer like a piping pot of New Orleans jambalaya. I backtracked by her booth, pretending to consider purchasing a purple and gold dashiki from the booth next to hers. I lifted my head slowly, measuring her gaze, conjuring a line in my head that would grab her in the first six words. She glared at me, almost daringly, a challenge I found irresistible. I nodded, hoping she'd say something. Because if she didn't I was taking my ass home, along with my fantasies and the six-pack of designer beer chilling patiently in my ice chest. I'd sit in the bathtub and dream about her. Picture her there with me. Me pouring lavender oil and cherry wine into the water. Letting the stream of the faucet flow to that spot on her silk, just above the pearl.

She nodded her head and that was the permission I needed to enter. My ego kicked in. My fantasy expanded as I pimp-strolled over to her booth humming a blues song under my breath: *I bet she likes to be loved slow/kissed long and steady/ this wild afrique woman/nothing but moans for music/no jazz or blues/no damn rules/just us moaning an original tune/a song for the rest of our life/a song slow and steady/the dog-gone truth/the dog-gone truth.* I kept walking and humming. Seemed like a million years went by. I tried my best to pretend that the pounding in my heart wasn't about to expose what was going through my mind.

"The African dolls are seventy-five dollars, the necklaces are twenty and up. Oh yeah, I do psychic readings too. The cost is a love offering of at least twenty-five dollars." Her deep velvety New York accent swam from her throat and lodged itself in my temple. I shook my head back and forth so that I could beam back to the moment.

"That was the nicest invitation to spend my hard-earned money I have ever received. Wrap up that necklace with the ankh in the middle. I'll take that one too—the one to the left of it with the amber stone." Yeah. I had a few dollars for Ms. Lady. Enough to back up the smooth mack I was getting ready to drop on this syrupy sister.

"And how much does it cost to take you to dinner?"

That was more than six words. But it didn't matter because it seemed to work. She smiled and I realized that what I thought was a cavity was a diamond in one of her front teeth. Sistah must have southern roots.

Then she answered, "Dinner? I'm a vegetarian. Do you like tofu?"

Shit, I was thinking about tossing this lovely over some barbecue ribs and potato salad and here she was talking about tofu. Hell, bud I'd eat a bowl of slimy okra to have a shot at her fine round ass. She ran her tongue across the pillows of her lips and began nervously arranging and rearranging the wares on her table. I was close to having her. I inched a bit closer so that I could inhale the sandalwood and ylang-ylang seeping from her skin. She reclined back in the folding chair and let a tiny bounce escape from her legs. That was the deal-clincher. Now I had to taste some of that perfume.

"Yeah, tofu's my favorite. I became a vegetarian about... oh, six months ago. May I ask what your name is?"

"Sojourner Maxwell. And you?"

Sojourner. Sistah has to be conscious calling herself Sojourner. "I'm Tommy. Tommy Williamson. My friends call me Tee. I live here in L.A., but I was born in Louisiana. The Big Easy, you know."

"New Orleans, huh? Home of the Voodoo Queen, Marie Laveau. Do you do voodoo, Tommy."

"I know enough to know that it's real, but I don't practice."

"That's too bad. Voodoo is some powerful shit."

Now she was scaring me. I mean, everybody knows a little something, even if it ain't nothing but how your grandmother used to cure a cold by placing raw onions under your armpits for twenty-four hours. But actually practicing voodoo was different.

"Some of those root doctors have the wrong intentions," I said, trying to see what she thought about folks who do wrong with that stuff.

"That's not voodoo, that's hoodoo. That's something the white man conjured up to demonize African religions."

I was slightly relieved. "Oh, OK, so you don't believe in hurting anybody?" It was a question but it came out like a statement. She never answered me. But I felt better just putting it out there.

"What time would you like to have dinner?" I asked, trying to close the deal.

"Did I say I was going to dinner with you?"

I played her game and didn't answer.

"I'll be done here at six o'clock. There's a restaurant called Mother's in West L.A. that's really nice. Have you been there before?"

"Am I picking you up?"

"Depends. Where do you live?" Before I could answer she said, "I tell you what, let's meet at the restaurant at seven, before the dinner rush."

"Cool. I'll see you at seven, Sojourner." I leaned over and kissed her on the cheek. The light sweat covering her cheek and her translucent face powder coated my lips. My legs were trembling when I straightened up.

She blushed and batted her eyes. "See you at seven, Tommy."

I could barely enjoy the festival after meeting Sojourner. The taste of her skin simply refused to leave my lips. After listening to two bands, I packed up and went home. I showered, spruced up the pad in case I got lucky, and made my way to Mother's. Luckily, it wasn't hard to find. When I arrived, Sojourner had a little surprise for me.

She was sitting at a table with another woman. She was a tad shorter than Sojourner, but wore the same Afrocentric garb. The smell of sandalwood hit me at the door, and once again I was intrigued. Sojourner rose and hugged me, her ample breasts smashing into my chest, causing friction between my legs. Her friend's name was Rhonda. She just happened to be dining there tonight, and of course Sojourner couldn't let her eat dinner alone.

We had a glib dinner and discussed everything from world politics to entertainment gossip. I was still hungry after eating a ton of whatever they ordered. Sojourner suggested that I try the sweet potato pie. The waitress brought me a huge slice, warm right out of the oven, with an overflowing scoop of vanilla yogurt. It was delectable, the best thing on the menu.

After our rabbity dinner we decided to go back to my place. I'd bragged about my jazz collection during dinner and Sojourner said she'd love to listen to some of her old favorites. Much to my dismay, Rhonda tagged along. As we loaded into the car, Rhonda dragged her breasts across my back as she eased into the back seat. Her thick nipples sent chills up my back. Damn, maybe this was going to be my lucky night. Two for one. It couldn't get any better than that.

I put on some Miles to kick off the party, then merged into Billie, slid into Thelonious, and finally settled into some Cassandra. I poured the sistahs an eclectic mixture of sparkling water, fruit juice, and herbal extracts designed to relax our minds and energize our bodies. The perfect aphrodisiac.

"This shit is good! What's it called again? Ame?" Sojourner asked me.

"It's pronounced 'Ah-may.' I'm glad you like it."

"Do you have any reefa?" Rhonda asked.

"I might be able to scrape a little something off of the bottom of the shoebox."

I went to my bedroom and checked my stash. I had just enough for one thin joint. Excited and nervous about the night's possibilities, I took nearly fifteen minutes to gather the leaves and separate them from the dust and seeds in the shoebox. I sealed the cigarette paper with my saliva and let it dry in the breeze of my motion. I came back to the living room with the reed between my lips.

I was trapped in my doorway, frozen by the sight of Sojourner and Rhonda engaging in one of the most passionate tongue kisses I had ever witnessed. Their tongues danced a song of sensual thirst. They flickered hard and solid, back and forth against each other. Rhonda's hands were gently pulling and twisting Sojourner's nipples. Sojourner's back was arched, her dress above her knees, exposing her honey-cinnamon thighs. When Rhonda slithered her hand up Sojourner's dress, I cleared my throat to let them know they weren't alone.

Rhonda came over to me, turned around with her back facing my front, and slid her ass backward into my crouch. She ground her backside into me in a swirling motion. Sojourner joined Rhonda in front of me, politely edging her to the side so that she could take over. She took the joint from my mouth and lit it. The smoke unfurled from her lips as she inhaled it into her nose and back to her mouth again. She stuck it in my mouth and I took a long drag, taking measures to ensure that the mellow-yellow took me to where I wanted to go.

Rhonda was next. She stuck the jay in Sojourner's mouth so that she could blow her an old-school charge. Sojourner simultaneously let the straps to her dress drift off her shoulders. Her thick mountains bounced forward, happy to be released. Drops of saliva dripped from the corner of my mouth as I took her nipples onto my tongue and sucked them like the last flesh of a succulent mango. I embraced her full, round ass with my hands and pulled her to me. She wrapped one of her glorious thighs around me and slammed her pelvis into mine. I damn near came, but I wanted to share that moment with her, so I held back until I could get her where I wanted her.

The three of us floated into my bedroom, shedding the rest of our clothing as we traveled. I immediately made Sojourner straddle my face while I sucked her into oblivion. Her clit swelled like an angry ocean and crashed onto my lips, creating its own shore. I slid two hungry fingers in and out of Rhonda's sweltering oven. I felt her orgasm coming so I stopped licking Sojourner and made Rhonda get on board. I locked Rhonda's pearl in between the small gap I was famous for. I sucked her lightly first, then built to a vibrating pulse that made her scream as her body shuttered with satisfaction. She rolled off my face, her limp body glimmering with beads of sweat.

Now Sojourner was back for more. I turned her over on her stomach, made her lie across my lap, and spanked her ass while I fingered her volcanic hole with slow precision. When I had her where I wanted her I commanded her to get on all fours. I slid into her and became completely enveloped by her warmth. I spanked her ass hard while I slid in and out of her. The impact of the slaps on her ass vibrated down to her clit. It was driving her crazy and I knew it, but we were helpless to stop. Rhonda licked and sucked my back while I fingered her ass gently. She began to press herself into my ass, stimulating her pearl again. I felt both of them ready to cum again so I took it to the next stage and began loving them with a ferocity that drove them to tears and screams at the same time. I came right along with them, my clitoris quaking like a five-point-four. Miles' horn screamed along with the three of us as we climaxed together.

Sojourner unhooked the strap to my chocolate-colored

dildo and laid it to the side. She pushed me down on my back. Her eyes promised to thank me profusely for making her feel so good. She placed her lips firmly around my already throbbing clit. Knowing I was sensitive, she simply licked me like a baby kitten until I found my second fire. When I could stand no more I spread my legs like wings and let her take me out of my body into her orbit. And there were no more secrets between us. That night became a story for the stars and the moon. No one but the sky would ever tell it. Spent and intoxicated by our intense loving, we lay together cooled by the summer breeze, connected by a three-way spoon.

On Sojourner's backside, right at the bottom of her spine, I noticed a tattoo. When I asked her about it she rubbed it with her fingertips and said, "That is the Voudoun symbol for love. It represents Erzulie, the goddess of love. I asked her to send me a lover today, and when I saw you I knew she'd answered my prayers."

All I could do was laugh. I'd been turned out by a voodoo woman and her distant lover. I guess I wasn't such a mack daddy after all. Before we got dressed, I took Sojourner into my closet and showed her my shrine to Erzulie. Her eyes bulged out in sheer surprise.

"So, my love," I said, "who would you say conjured who?"

Shared Heat
Tracy Price-Thompson

This desert night, like all the others before it, is scalding. Lingering waves of humidity drift across the diamond-lit sky and create a kaleidoscope of sparkling movement. My cocoa-colored military-issue T-shirt is molded to my cinnamon frame; the salt of my moisture clings to my skin and pools between my unbound breasts before forming a puddle in the sloping well of my navel.

We are at war, and fraternization is strictly forbidden in this strange land. Yours is an infantry combat unit, and there are no female troops in this border region. The landscape is witness to little activity save for the desert peddlers draped in flowing robes and light headdress, their women covered from head to toe in seeming miles of sheer material, their curious eyes mere slits behind dark, Arabian folds.

As America's first female combat photographer I consider these feeble attempts at sexual suppression among the troops absurd, and though my feet are broiling and my clothing damp, I watch closely as you trudge valiantly ahead of your riflemen through the shifting sand. Your broad shoulders are starched-straight and ramrod; there is power in your lengthy stride. My breathing is strained and heavy as your muscular buttocks flex visibly through the fabric of your uniform, their curvature sending carnal desire pumping deliciously through my veins, ebbing and flowing with the pounding of my heart.

Nearing the perimeter of our encampment, you command us to trickle single-file through the maze of concrete barricades. From the dark walls of a bunker emerges a terrified sentinel. He barks a verbal challenge and you respond with the appropriate password.

Blackness descends and blankets the desert floor as we enter the compound. Your men are relieved to be back at camp, their backs bent with exhaustion, heavily laden with smoldering weapons of death, weary after toiling away in the pliant sand of this heat-filled crevice of the earth.

Regretful that our night's work of probing and reconnoitering has come to a close, I free the tangle of braids from my banded ponytail. I allow them to spill unfettered down my back and sigh in frustration as you march past me without a sideways glance, your chin prominently chiseled in profile. You gather your maps and radios to prepare for the night's briefing, and I am left alone to return to the solitude of my sleeping tent.

It has been several weeks since I replaced an aging Brit whose nerves finally wore out after months of witnessing the death and carnage of battle after bloody battle. Weeks for me, but long months for you and your men. I force myself to quiet the clicking shutters of my camera, to cease the endless snapshots required of me. My job is to satisfy the public's shameless bloodlust while immortalizing the essence of this desert war.

You balked at my presence as I rode into your camp, my arms overflowing with equipment, my press credentials dangling between my breasts.

A female, you spat bitterly, in the midst of hundreds of war-weary fighting men. *She will cause distraction,* you warned. *She will require special consideration. She will bear watching.*

You refused to address me, yet through the voice of your First Sergeant you isolated my sleeping tent. You forbade me entrance to the bivouac area and banished me to the perimeters of the operation, far away from the searching eyes and midnight dreams of the hundreds of combat-worn, virile young men.

This is not an easy assignment for you, a black infantry-commander. A leader of troops, you sleep in harm's way. Each casualty is like a hot knife plunged into your gut. Every soldier blasted to bits by land mines and hand grenades is your very own son. Death creeps nearer each time a missile explodes into the dark night, and danger lurks in every rustle of the wind, prowls in cryptic shifts of the sand.

It is only during these night reconnoiters, while the lens of my camera records and bears witness to the scores of broken bodies scattered across the sand, that I am bid entrance to your world. Unlike mine, your job is to fight and to die, and it is a near-certain death, this occupation of yours. Yet, as with me, the uncertainty of survival has rendered you ravenous, held you hostage from your desires.

We do not exchange words, you and I. Your ivory teeth flash like lightning against the midnight of your skin as you pretend not to notice me. The curly hairs teasing your upper lip dismiss me as you bark orders at your men, life-or-death tension making your words terse, causing your brow to furl and unfurl in a series of fierce scowls.

I am not deceived. I notice how your eyes, shielded by dark lashes, seem to suckle from me. To drink from my ebony curves of life. I take my fill from you as well, wondering what it would be like to drown in the quicksand of your love. My nose detects the scent of your manhood. My eyes roam over the telltale rising that occurs in your groin whenever I am near, and I smile inwardly as I bide my time.

Of course you want me. As do your men.

And I delight in my power. My delta surges. My nipples strain. Mine is the only dripping pussy within endless miles of ravaged sand, and desperate hands bearing bands of gold grope my high breasts, cup the subtle sweetness of my rolling hips. Hot promises of unprecedented passion find their way to my ears from the pleading lips of Deon, Daryl, David, and Tyrone.

Yet, of the hundreds of eager organs awaiting my command, for me there is only yours. In you I sense the greater need, and it is you I dream of. Dreams of steamy illusion, only to awaken alone in my secluded tent, drenched beneath the broiling desert sun, the phantom of your manhood still throbbing wickedly between my lonely thighs, your ghostly kiss still burning against the swell of my brown breasts.

Forbidden to enter your area of operations, I cloak myself in the shadows of the mess tent and listen to your briefing as your face turns to steel. Your men squat before you in a semicircle, and the First Sergeant's hands shake as he reads the combat orders sent down from your higher command.

You will depart at o-dark-thirty. The first rays of the Southwest Asian sun will find you probing far behind battle lines, deep in the belly of enemy territory where your men will attempt to accomplish a mission impossible.

Fucking suicide. The slight breeze lifts the growled words from your full lips and lights them upon my ears. The last outfit to attempt such a breach had been slaughtered. Color photos bore witness to a bloodsoaked desert floor strewn with bodies, naked and stripped of glory. The First Sergeant crumples the orders in his fist and spits. Some dickhead back in Washington is sending flesh-and-bone men in where even armored equipment would be blown to bits.

I tremble at his apprehension. It is real and palpable even from this distance.

There will be no cameras on this mission, you declare emphatically, your onyx eyes burning through the black shadows and piercing my hiding place. *There will be no women.*

Panic snatches at my throat and claws my belly. Artillery fire resounds in the distance. My boot-clad feet sink into the sand. The First Sergeant speaks the truth: War is a deadly game. A game played for keeps. The stakes are high. The booty is life, the punishment a bloody death. The thought of you slipping into the stars, perhaps never to return, is unbearable. I cannot allow you to go into battle without a measure of protection. My unrequited midnight dreams leave my loins slick and wet and fill me with agony.

This could be it.

Your last night.

Then tonight will be different, I vow. Tonight, instead of the coarse blankets scraping at our centers, there will be flesh upon flesh. Bone against bone.

My mind races as you give your men the order to disperse. Fear and tension roll off their unwashed bodies and clog the stagnant air. They understand the impending peril and are not ashamed to show their fear.

Fear is good, I think. Fear can keep you alive.

But as I watch you watching them, there is something greater than fear in your eyes. A desperate something that resembles anguish as you study their retreating backs. Some stride into the night with instructions to guard the perimeter. More retreat to their foxholes to clean weapons. Others, taking advantage of the calm before the storm, drag themselves through the sand to their makeshift homes, row upon row of camouflaged mounds in the sandy tent city.

You remain behind, your posture pensive, an air of

exhausted loneliness surrounding you. Responsibility lands like a brick and burrows into your gut. Their lives are in your hands.

A sole figure silhouetted against the electrified sky, you rise to your feet and momentarily gaze up at the stars. As you stretch your arms toward the heavens, the heavy muscles in your back coil and rope lazily beneath your damp shirt. My loins leak a sudden, desperate passion and I collapse against the cloth of the mess tent and hold my breath. My heart thumps madly beneath my breasts, my thighs clench and unclench, the delta between them melting and molding into a tiny throbbing triangle.

My fingers find my breasts, my nipples already as stiff as stone. I am fascinated as you turn the long structure of your body and stride into the camel-colored folds of your sleeping tent, six months of pent-up fear, uncertainty, and desire in your step. My eyes remain glued to the spot where you have just been, as my hands hurriedly undo the buttons on my chocolate chip–patterned trousers.

I am powerless as I delve into my own wetness, my fingers hard and exacting as I probe my slippery folds. I find my spot and rub and massage until I pant aloud. I imagine that my gliding fingers belong to you, my wetness a by-product of our love. I fuck myself furiously, rocking my solitary hips back and forth across the mound of my own fist, bringing myself to the brink time after time, until finally a rocket explodes in my groin and tiny pellets of combustion scorch my breasts.

As I gaze up at the audience of stars, I am filled with heat, yet I remain empty. My breasts rise and fall as my breathing slows. Minutes fly by as I fight to quell the rising tide in my gluttonous cavern. My need has not yet been sated.

I grow more determined.

There is something I must give you: a talisman of sorts. A rabbit's foot, a sow's ear, a monkey's lip.

I move closer to the doorway through which you have disappeared.

Trembling fingers secure the tent flaps behind me as I slip into the darkness of your desert home. Moonlight filters in from the slit in the roof, and I marvel at your perfection as I kick off my boots and tear at my clothing. Bathed in silver, your form is outlined on the low cot, tangled and ensnared in the olive-drab sleeping bag.

Mortar rounds explode to the east as I tiptoe through the yielding sand and slide in beside you, my thighs draping over yours as I snuggle into the hard lines of your physique. You stir gently but do not awaken. Heat radiates from my skin as I move closer, desperate to be one with you.

My hand snakes lazily across your chest, fingers tangling in the curls that cover your smooth brown skin. I drag my fingers lower and find your navel, gently rubbing around its soft perimeter. I feel an inferno glowing from its center and bursting from your groin, and my hand plunges there like a heat-seeking missile.

I search gingerly.

Your manhood is regal. Proud and defiant. It lurches at my contact, the thick veins bringing sweet delight to my wandering fingers. I wrap my hand around your thickness, and tiny volts of electricity radiate from my palm to the tips of my breasts. My nipples harden and reach outward.

I grasp the crest of your beautiful black penis and glide my hand over the mushroom-shaped head. My hand stops just beneath the swollen crown and I squeeze gently. Your body stiffens and you moan softly in your sleep. Gently, I pump up and down, squeezing softly each time I reach the top of your shaft.

I find your heavy balls and fondle and massage them both with one hand. Slowly, your hips begin to gyrate, making deep fucking motions into my moist palm. I slide my body against you, and your legs move apart. I nestle down in the V between your thighs and make myself comfortable. I lick your left nipple and then greedily begin to suckle, making hectic swirls with my tongue and biting gently as I pull your tiny knob into my mouth.

Your arms close around me, gripping me firmly as you pump your steel into the softness of my stomach. I break the contact and slide down your body, my tongue leaving a wet trail on the landscape of your belly and chest.

The heavy scent of your manhood rises to meet me and my pussy begins to drip. I ignore the explosive echoes of cannon fodder and bury my nose in your pubic hair, then slide further down into your heaven. I part your thighs a bit wider, then cup your balls gently in my hands. I lick first one, then the other, before opening my mouth to invite them both inside. I suck your balls like precious candy as I grip the extra-hard shaft of your penis. Your moans tell me just how much you like my technique, and I renew my motions with vigor.

Suddenly, I release your heavy sac and lower my wet mouth over the head of your black serpent. You groan deeply as my boiling cave descends like black lava over your eager, pulsating shaft. I wrap my full lips firmly around the base, and suck and slurp greedily as I take six, seven, eight, then all nine inches down my throat and bathe it lovingly with my soft tongue.

I sigh. The sensation of your throbbing manhood, vibrating and pushing at the back of my throat, is like no other. I pull back a bit and leave inch by inch of it exposed to the naked air, then I slam my head back down and make hot circular motions as I play tongue games with the main vein running along its side. I slurp and nibble and suck until your hips buck wildly and you fuck my mouth as if it were a pussy. I can feel your cum building and swirling along toward an explosion, and I squeeze hard with one hand and rub your ass with the other.

You almost scream with pleasure as you rock back and forth into my mouth. I rub my legs together, the slippery cream of my pussy sliding down my thighs. Suddenly you pull your self from my mouth and gather me up to face you. Your tongue now probes where your penis has just been, and we share the sweet taste of your manliness between us. Your fingers find my dripping center and you gently part the lips and rub my clit, dipping down into my silky pot of love and bringing the moisture up to slather my growing bud.

I sigh deeply and spread my legs wider. You lay me back and kiss each of my erect nipples. You cup my breasts in your hand and rub and knead them as if they are two beautiful brown babies. With one hand you stoke my heat and slide your fingers in and out of my wet sheath, and with the other you squeeze my breasts while you lick my thick nipples.

I almost faint when you plunge your head lower and cover me with your nibbling lips. The sensation is far too exquisite and I fight you momentarily, unable to bear such direct pleasure. You push me past that point, gently licking my mound with building pressure on my clit. Every few seconds you reach down with your tongue and dip inside, gathering my juices and rubbing them all over my clit. I squeeze my thighs together and fuck at your face, my legs thrashing wildly from pleasure.

You lick my slit, up and down, deeply inserting your tongue, then withdrawing it and swirling about my clit and back and forth and back and forth and back and forth. I grab your head and push your face deeper as my orgasm bursts forth from me in a long flood of liquid that you lick and suck and swallow with joy. I purr like a kitten as my bottom rubs against the coarse cot and I cup and squeeze my own breasts in satisfaction. You kiss each of my thighs, then slide your body up to mine.

The scent of gunpowder rides the tails of a leftover breeze, and I glimpse your erection in the shadows of the moonlight and shiver. Its majestic beauty is undeniably powerful and alluring. Somehow, as you suckled from me, your regal weapon has grown an additional two inches, and it now spits white love from its tip and throbs menacingly as it approaches my soft brown hole. I bite my lip as you enter me with one massive thrust, pushing every bit of your thick hard meat into me at once.

Pleasure waves explode in my womb as you fill me. I groan as you pound and push and buck wildly into my gaping softness, your thrust so powerful and long and hard that your balls slap my ass wetly each time the tip of your penis rams my womb. My legs are spread wide enough to split as you grab my ass with both hands, lift me slightly from the cot, and burrow within me so hard and so deep I almost cry from the intense pleasure-pain. I rub your ass with both hands and hold on tight as you ride me, sliding and slamming in and out. My wetness splashes against your thighs. Our hairs tangle and mingle as my eager mound rises up to meet you, waves of cum soaking your pounding organ.

You moan in ecstasy as you take a swim in the hot pool of my honey, splashing around madly, pushing deeply and withdrawing. Your balls tighten; your anus pulsates; my teeth rake across your nipples. My hands are slapping your ass, clenching and drawing you further and further and deeper until you pound and thrust even harder, your chest crushing the pillows of my breast. My pussy is sliding hot and wet up your shaft. My thighs clench and relax, clench and relax as you fuck me and I fuck back. Then an explosion ignites from you, sending hot waves spiraling up your tube and shooting like lava out the tip of your shaft.

Your roar eclipses the desert moon as you cast your burning wetness into the softness of my well. We hold each other tightly as shock waves curl our toes, harden our nipples, drench us in blessed sweat, and extinguish our shared heat.

What seems like hours later, our breathing finally slows and you kiss me gently and smile, your eyes shining like black diamonds. Your manhood growls its satisfaction and I smile back and kiss each of your eyelids, searing your features upon my memory; then I slip from your arms and retrieve my clothing and quietly depart.

We do not speak, you and I, and we never will. Yet, as I steal away beneath the bright Arabian stars, our eyes form a covenant: a promise made possible due to the binding of our flesh and the heat we shared on the platform of your desert bed. Silently, your eyes accept your fate as they thank me for the gift of my loins, your armor and your shield, to fortify and strengthen me and to ward off all danger.

My eyes hold the promise of remembrance as I vow to hold tight to the precious pool you deposited deeply in my womb. To hold tight to the essence of you, a brave black leader of men, who in the darkness of night planted his seed with a queen, and, in return, was inoculated with enduring life in the broiling hot theater of death.

Magick
folade mondisa speaks-love

"pull up your skirt   i want your seaweed
move your panties to the side
show me   the hair under your arms
you haven't shaved have you   don't break
my heart and tell me you shaved again
pull up your shirt so i can   smell the musk   your hair
traps in   farther   more   tell me   you want me   to swim
beneath   your wet seaweed
you smell so fucking good   your scent   is so intoxicating"

a jar of honey a teaspoon of her blood   will heal him
in my own mind   the elements became a reincarnated thing
one october evening....
there is an old voodoo spell   if a woman   drops   as
little   as a teaspoon   of her
blood into   a man's tea   it is said   that she will never
leave his head that he will never leave   her
he'll always   want   her triangle   the wet sweet   the
middle but this spell   is for the fool

who won't drink   the blood   willingly
for the fool who doesn't   know
the power   of her honey   will heal him
*   (these are things i know)*

with all my intuition   you   like an apparition
mysteriously   appeared before me
moon conjured you   out of nowhere   but i've known   you
ram lover
remember   the magical way
your oculus disappears into your orgasm   the jerk
your deflational heaviness   descending me

pull up my sleeves   wrap your fingers around   my intuition

    you ask, "are you a witch?"

my divining plate   would narrate omens
when we fuck waves thunder

when i am swimming   when i am casting cowries with other
sirens   when i am a rockfish skipping stones across
the water's surface   and feel   the pounce of your feet
upon earth
near me i celebrate you

he adores hair   rubs his nose his eyes his mouth and tongue
in mine   in any crevice
that grows hair   that is where he dwells   where his head
moves in a back-and-forth motion
like there is jazz flowing from those places
he adores hair   asks me   "do you wonder why i love hair so
much   but shave the hair*
from my cock?"   *"no absolutely not"   i tell him   i know*

that he shaves
his own hair   to be closer to mine but there are times when
he is out of me   when i cannot   access him   my legs gyrate
openings go into convulsions cunt hallucinates   organs
kick and scream my openings pour   heels pound floor like
hands to jembe   my heart turns sensory   to find him my
pheromones pant   they need water   I need breath   need
for him to dwell in my entry   why?
because each time we fuck   he heals me

i ask,   "what turns you on?"   he answers, "the hunt"

a long journey a huge organ   a pelvic area   will stagger

i want to bring you toys   i want to tie you up   i want to
blindfold you   i want to bring food
i want to eat on you   i want to eat from you   i want to
eat you   i want to bring you toys   battery toys   fruit toys
cream   i want to bring you a living breathing toy that talks i
want to watch you lick her   i want to watch her lick you   i
want to see your body move
with a woman's body   i want her to eat your pussy while
your lips are wrapped around my dick   you suck good dick
yeah   you definitely suck good dick   would you object
to the toy   the living breathing toy   the female toy   would
you object kamania?

oil rests on his skin   line my tongue devoted to   the
bittersweet of it   hovering over me
he feels like rain   he is a lion   mane   wide mouth   the
beast in him echoes   through release   in the loud way   he
holds himself   there and bends to the side   and holds
himself in it   and straightens   into an ejaculation echo
the beast in him   descends and parallels me   prancing into

a whisper   he tells me he wants my breath   and tongues the
right hand crease   of my smile   he makes that place
the inverted prism of my organs
my mouth   comes   the veins in my neck   come   my throat
pants   spring is born in me

he asks me, "do men approach you?   often? how?   what
do they say?   how   do they look at you?   how   do
they respond?   where   do they think you're from?   do
you respond?   what do you say?   do   women approach
you?   how   often?   more   than men   or just as much?   i
thought   you said men don't   approach you that   often?
what do they say   about you?   mysterious?   it's very true
they share my observation   they detect the witch in you"

my   mystery be   coming   apparition

I whisper,
"why are you becoming   selective and cautious about my
energy?   what do you mean   it's too powerful?
why   are you becoming 'safe?'   why have you started
to fuck me on top   of the bed   instead   of   pulling back
the sheets? why don't   you hang my coat   in the closet
next to your clothes?   why
do you hang it from the door   neatly on a hanger   like it's
my apparition?   why do you fix the hang of the fabric?
why   do you straighten the collar?"
and then I scream, "why do you always smell the scarf
before   you place it carefully around the coat's neck?   why
don't you just hang it in the closet?   why   has the word
attached   become a curse?   why   the last few times i've
seen you   have you wrapped your hair   in red cotton?
why are you keeping your hair 'safe'
from my fingers?   lover, why?"

i celebrate   him by daily drinks of honey   open my
salivating mouth and drink the nectar
so it will ooze with my orgasm   slowly from between my
thighs   into his mouth
this is when his dick rises   climbs in him   squeezes out
through his teeth

he admits,   "i can't get rid of your scent   if i hang   your
coat with my shit   your smell permeates my shit   it hangs
in my locks   it stays   in my sheets   i think
your scent lives in the mattress   even after   the sheets are
changed   even after i shower   after days
you stay   here   you stay   with me on me   in me
i can't get rid of   your scent   driving me crazy   if i wish
days after we fuck   i can lick my mouth   and there   you
are   i daydream of you   i grab myself   you never leave
lover   your scent is the mantra   that lives   in my room"

(i make a mental note of it)

and he continues, "you move my root chakra   i'm not
moved easily kamania   you do something to me   you
are the source   in which I express my joy in passion and
sex   you are that place i travel to seek it all   you evoke
constant fantasies   of fucking you   i love to fuck you   it's
inebriating   you have such a powerful   appeal and   sweet
scent i'm not talking about your body oils
your frankincense   or your amber
tell me what i'm talking about   kamania   tell me you know
i'm talking about your pussy"

sandalwood in my mouth   your nipples tongue my lips

he explains,   "kamania   i don't go to a flower shop
expecting heavily scented flowers   cut from earth the
sweetest flowers   are living   you are a flower   a wild
bush   the most sweet-smelling   the most natural   you
are a wild   bee that flower   dress your waist in beads   i
want you   in a waistlet   with a strand of beads   that
goes down between your legs connects from your navel   to
your back   rubs against your clit   something soft
and comfortable   but erotic   would you wear that for
me kamania? dress your waist in beads to express your
sexuality—
to evoke it even more? ah   that's my girl   i'd love that"

he is like rain water
falling on my earth
masquerading as a bath
my legs writing a triangle
around his head I am an altar
everything is an altar he makes a feast
of my possessions his lips taking my cranberry blood
oh the prism tear he'd be rolling down my cheek had he a
second life
my body releasing my scent into his air he makes an altar of
me in the arms of earth

with curiosity and slurring words, he asks,   "so kamania
baby   tell me   are you heavy or do you not bleed that
much?   when was the last time you slept with someone
while you were on your period?   how does it smell right
now?   how does it taste?   sure you know you have it
right there with you   smell it   taste it   tell me   it smells
as sweet as it smelled   the other night?   when you literally
left a sweet taste in my mouth   oh baby you're killing me
do you want to   meet me   down the street   for a drink?"

four times now   your body has healed me   made me feel
like   a good night's sleep
a chamomile bath   a nature walk   baby   like aphrodite's
fruit   you make me
rain blue again   each night i fuck you   it snows   you fall to
my stomach   to my chest
to my mouth   this tongue   these hips   wait for the sky
to fall   i'm waiting   for the fifth time   so we can call up
divination
lying beside me   you pull off my panties   your dick   hard
skin
stretched   tight   cock standing straight   waiting to float
in my cycle   ready   remembering   how good it feels to
pull up my dress   undress my flesh   your dick shining   its
veins   protruding   my panties resting   over your
searching nose   your eyes close

he asks,   "baby, how are your panties so wet? don't you
have on a tampon?"

I answer, "yes and while you smell my panties   while you
inhale   my familiar scent reminding you   of who is down
there drowning there   i want you   to feel the moistness of
my panties' fabric   against your lips   against the beauty
mark   that rests   near the left crease   of the tip of your
mouth"

his lips?   they pout even when he is smiling   his mouth is
always happy   as if
he has stored the finest tastes upon his tongue   and is
celebrating a sweet palate orgasm they v   his top lip
meets the deep pierce of his bottom lip   i want to plant
the whole of me there i want to taste you   to feel the

132

sandalwood texture between your penis and ass   so i stretch
myself down   while painting your torso   with saliva   you
push   your hardness
to the back of my mouth   you penetrate my throat   and
move my hair   away watch
my tongue   your dick   slides in and out of my mouth
teasing you giving you   slow   fast   in deeper
but   i would curl up in the pyramid between his pecs
there   in that place
my hand fits perfectly   and inherently finds its way there
every time we fuck   every time we stroke   tongues
every time   there are nile waves   below the pyramid
that spread around his torso   his back dips   vertebrae
curves a graceful arch   his arms bend slightly   at his elbows
he holds them   as if to say,   "i'm ready for anything"
you   finger   my calyx   spread it open   pull out my cotton
throw it to the floor
turn me over and push   yourself inside me   i   tingle
from the feeling   of your dick entering   i cum around
you   stain the blanket   i soak   you swim   inside my
wetness

"kamania i want to taste you   open your legs"

you drink my blood   like a fetish   like a vampire
celebrate my moon ritual   healed like a good night's sleep
giving thanks for my blood   drink it like a deity   from my
body this altar
you take my sacrifice   you sacrifice   yourself to me
willingly
dear fetish   (these are things I know)
i am libation   before your mirror   i am a stream
of pink sepals in the carpet
i am a warm calyx   between your legs   i am lips that pull

you into me
like ladyfingers   i am the rosebush   whose wild smell
dwells at the base of your nose   i am pollinated stomach
flesh   after you come   i am shape shifted   bayou
twelve times a year   spring is flowering   to celebrate
my senses

i can turn a picnic into an orgy   celebrate my senses   sit
on the ground   feel earth masturbate my clitoris   now that
i've known you   my nose searches   for your scent
in heat i delve toward your flames   i am jupiter   with her
own sun
if my gods were ever angry   they are now dancing suns
when you read this letter
you will open   the smooth earth-colored envelope
and the reproductive organs
of a crossbred tulip   magenta pink with yellow birthmarks
will fall into you   two of its petals will find their way   to
your eyes first   your thick fingers   will take out the sweet
smell   there   i am reaching   in the middle   to touch you
which is inherent   reaching   remembering   knowing
seeing   tasting   smelling
the cranberry honey of my uterus
*   and that   don't seem   like voodoo   to me*

Talk to Me
Tara Betts

Let's not front. If it's good, cussing in bed is a given, just like smacking a substantial ass. I smile at the thought. I know now it was looking down into his face that made it unbearable. Nutmeg brown, framed by a clipped black beard and mustache around full lips, dreadlocks spread like an Afro-mandala around his head. I saw vulnerability in his face, but it was trapped behind a mouth that offered no syllables. The parting of his lips in a soft, slow gasp. The long fingers, the arching back, the rise of hips into mine. Each shift, each tremble culminated softly on his face.

But I couldn't understand why his silence bothered me. Why was I looking for words when his hands broke me into quivering spells? I mean, the man even makes dinner after a full day at work and kisses the back of my neck while I'm at the computer. He looks me in the eye as if I'm the world. It's not that I didn't trust him in spite of the quiet. I did. I just needed to hear the words. *Tell me what it feels like. Do you like it? I'm here, baby. Hold me. I love holding you. Oooooh, when you move like that, don't stop, don't, ooooh, you taste...damn, don't stop, can't let go, don't move.* But it wasn't happening.

So, I'm walking up the block with my keys in hand and I'm waiting to see his big old Kool-Aid grin. Just thinking about it pulls a throb from me. *Girl, baby girl, woman, what you doin' hot and wet like that? Damn.* Makes me want to cross my legs and stop to look up at the stars. Key in the lock, then I step into the hallway, up three short steps to the landing. Nag Champa sweetens the apartment. He's smiling and one of his locks points at me as if speaking for him. I reach my arms toward his outstretched smile. Far be it from me not to be, like, "Hey, ba'y, thought about you today."

"Really?" he answers. "Not too busy saving the world?"

"Always. Not enough time in the day."

"Well, sometimes we make time."

"Make time for what?" My lips curled into curlicues as I stretched the vowels. He knows I strain them with skills and volume when coaxed. OK, at least a little coaxing. OK, no fronting, not much coaxing at all. It's been days since I've heard that drop in his voice, as if the beat was riding in just a little heavier, as if it's made for my hip pockets.

Now we're sipping merlot, one glass, but it's not as sweet as kissing him for ten solid minutes. I know he sees me thinking just that, when my lips press into the glass rim. He looks like he's about to curl into the big reading chair with me until one of his long arms pulls me up, close to his chest.

"What's wrong with you, boy?" I smile that coy, teenage smile at him.

"Nothing," he says, smiling back. He's talking with his face. I don't hear any music, but I'm feeling the rhythm in this dance. I like the beat that leads us to the bedroom, peeling back our clothes like dried husks that can't hold the juicy flesh inside. The kisses don't end, don't stop. My skin is swelling from his lips. Each lock brushes me to shudders and I can't help hoping he will say something so that I can hear the sound of brother-voice I've grown accustomed to in these moments. I want his voice to push me over the crooked edges of my screams. *Yeah, baby. That's it. You feel so damn good. Damn, baby, you wet. You gonna come for me, baby? You gonna make some noise? Scare my neighbors?*

My response breaks through in half question/half moan. "What, baby?" I'm hoping I heard him say it 'cause it was sounding too good in my head. He shakes his head *no* without stopping, and shatters the fantasy. His eyes are closed, and I'm tempted to rock even faster until they pop wide open. I'm waiting for the honey-dipped bass to fall into my ears. No words. I'm pent up with goddamn wondering when the whispers will flow. Say something, shit.

He's nothing but lean. Eyes closed as his head rocks back and forth against the pillow. Fingers clasped over our heads. His flat, firm stomach forms a *V* at his hips where tiny, fine, clustered hairs line their way into tickling my stomach. He's opening his mouth so that I see the white of his square teeth mocking the moonlight that peeks through slanted blinds. *I feel you squeezing me. God, you're wet. You know I love you. You know you can do whatever you want, baby. Whatever. Shiiitt....*

He still hasn't spoken. But his breath is keeping time with some go-go song and I can't remember the title. I don't even want to recall. Egyptian musk is clinging to his neck like my mouth is. His hand brushes behind my ear and a twitch blooms into a lotus of shock across my back. He starts rubbing my ass with the sheets. Now, why did he have to do that?

So I start. "Damn you. Why does your dick have to be so good? You know how bad I wanted this. This shit is like prayer. You gonna give me what I want? Baby?"

Every word's a stutter-step. I clamp onto him and we are both pushing with as much speed and force as our bones will allow. I think I hear his mouth open. I know what finally comes out. I hear, "Yes, baby. Yessss...."

Something crashes inside me. A tidal wave rushes up my thighs, my spine, my shoulders. The tremors burst into citrus-colored fans underneath my eyelids. Then a scream finally crashes out of my mouth and into the dark. When we collapse, press skin to skin, we are breathless. We are, again, silent. Without words.

Shout
Robin G. White

It seems like it took me forever to get here. One solid year of watching Miss Mavis Dupree. Sister Mavis Dupree, that is. One solid year. Mm-mmm. What a woman. Every Sunday I, Marva L. Malcomb, do the praise and worship hour at the Divine Deliverance Tabernacle. Oh, we really get the spirit moving. Sister Etta Wrigley leads the Jubilee chorus in their weekly shoutfest as I get things going with my organ. My fingers fly across those keys while my feet pump the pedals. It's not an easy thing to do unless you're doin' it for the Lord like I am.

Some Sundays I can hit it just right as Sister Wrigley shouts, "Put your hands together for Jesus. Let your praises be heard in the heavens. Hallelujah! Lift your voices and let me hear an Amen. I said, lift those voices of praise. In the name of Jesus, In the name of Jesus, We have a victory...." The whole congregation joins in clapping and singing while I'm just a playin' on that organ.

Well, this one particular Sunday, about a year ago, is when Sister Mavis Dupree came to join us. I noticed her right off because of her height. Not too many folks can be six foot two and not be noticed, especially not a woman like Sister Mavis. No, no. Not like Sister Mavis. She stood off to herself on the left side of the church looking a little lost and quiet. She wore a long plain skirt and blouse. Her hair was neatly pulled back and held with a clip. Pretty, but plain.

We were in the middle of praise when the usher seated her in the midst of Sister Beulah's crew. They were rocking and swaying and you knew it was getting ready to hit the pitch when Brother Marcus began to jog. He jogged first across the front of the church and then back. Well, that just got those sisters riled up 'cause the next thing you knew three or four of them had joined him, and Sister Martine had started with the cries. "Oh, Jesus. Yes, Lord. My God, my God. Oh. Oh. Oh. Yes, Jesus. Oh, yes, Jesus. Oh. Oh. Oh. Jesus, Jesus, Jesus. Oh, Jesus, Jesus, Jesus." The attendants came and caught her just as she swooned.

Brother Bishop had joined in the fray and was now jumping straight up and down in place. This started his whole row going. I was moving my fingers up and down the keyboard, punctuating every percussive bass note I could find right in beat with Lloyd Jr. on the congas. The Jubilee singers took their cue, "I'm in my Father's house, I dance I sing I shout. I love to give Him praise and bless His Holy Name. Shout, Shout, Shout. Dance, Dance, Dance. Sing, Sing, Sing. And bless His Holy Name." Sister Wrigley raised her skirt and did a little step. Brother Richard grabbed a tambourine as Sister Jean worked over the bass guitar. Hallelujahs went up everywhere.

Out of the corner of my eye, I could see her hands clapping. She bent over and put her Bible and purse on the seat behind her. The crowd was pulsating. Brother Edwards and his grinnin' self edged over toward her. That dog. If it wore a dress he just had to sniff under it. But she was gone.

She moved forward in the midst of the commotion and threw her head back. Her arms fell to the side and her feet started dancing. Her torso trembled as she submitted to the Holy Ghost's taking her shaking and dancing all the way from one side of the church to the other. The hair in that neatly pinned bun just let itself loose. Back and forth she leaned, first one way then the other, her body surrendering to that good gladness, that happy dance. Her hips moved in time with the music, grinding and gyrating. Her pelvis pumping and pushing that fine behind back and forth.

And all the while I was playing. Oh, man, was I playing. I could feel my behind sliding from one end of the bench to the other, feet pumping away at the pedals, my fingers stroking those ivory keys with deliberate measure, my tongue licking my lips. I locked onto her step and moved faster and faster as the congregation's fervor grew to a collective pitch. No one was seated. Some twelve hundred folks were shouting, "Hallelujah, Praise Jesus, Thank you Father, Yes Lord." But above it all I could hear her voice. "Yes, Jesus," she shouted. "Yes, Jesus. Oh, God, Yes, Jesus!"

My body was trembling, twitching. I could feel the burn in my thighs as I pounded those pedals harder with my feet. My throat became dry as I sucked in short breaths between the hiss of the "Yes, Jesus, Oh, yes, Jesus," moaning between my lips. My bottom felt on fire. As I continued to bounce along the bench my cheek muscles contracted with each syncopated beat. I began to lose the rhythm as the all-too-familiar explosion edged its way to the surface. The strain showed on my face. I slowed the rhythm of my music. And God's people followed suit. Sister Mavis collapsed in her pew as she turned to wink and smile at me.

Till that moment I'd thought I'd experienced this by myself. But there she was, her smile radiating a familiar afterglow. Tendril strands of hair curled about her ears and neck, wove around her collar, and fell between the folds of her blouse, caressing her cleavage. I had to know her.

Throughout the service I caught myself watching her demure beauty recollecting itself from the earlier release. Each exquisite movement was in itself a distraction. My mind raced. What had the wink meant? Had she felt me as I had felt her? Or was she merely thanking my spirit for moving hers? I refocused my thoughts on the day's lesson and back to my duties as organist.

My legs still ached from the earlier workout. Nearly an hour had passed since service ended. Pastor congratulated me on my "spirited playing" and joked about how I continued to raise the bar for him to inspire the congregation. I nodded and smiled, thinking of the particular congregant who had inspired my playing.

I rushed out of the church, knowing in my heart that she had already gone. I looked to the lot across the street and my heart sank. My car was the only one there. I gathered the strap of my music bag, slung it over my shoulder, and headed toward the foot of the stairs and the street. As I moved toward the curb, I lowered my head and bemoaned the lost opportunity. A horn blared and chased away my reverie. I looked up in time to catch a glance of Miss Mavis Dupree, her slender arm waving through the driver's side window of the silver Mustang as it roared by. I floated two feet off the ground to my car and winged my way home.

The following Sunday came after an excruciatingly slow week. Every morning I rose counting the days to Sunday's return. And when it finally arrived, I was on the steps of the church at seven for the eight A.M. service. By 9:45 I was frantically searching the burgeoning crowd for Miss Mavis's face. She didn't disappoint me. Again, she sat on the left side of the church. Her hair was pulled back and pinned in the same tight bun. Her skirt, long and unadorned, accentuated the

A-line of her frame. Her heels added two inches to her height.

I started the music off slowly, the melodies framed by sweet harmonies above and below. "Jesus on the main line…" Sister Eveline, the soloist, crooned dramatically as the choir chimed in, "Tell him what you want…." The crowd was being massaged. Their toes were tapping, fingers popping, heads bopping. Sister Beulah's crew began clapping, snapping, and tapping. Sister Wrigley began her step; Brother Edwards wandered over to some unsuspecting pretty young thang in a long, flower-print dress.

I took it up a notch and gave Sister Martine her cue. The attendants rushed, fans in hand, to her side. Lloyd Jr. grabbed hold of those congas and beat the black right out of them. It was *on*. My bass notes dueled with his drums and matched Sister Jean's bass guitar. Sister Etta Wrigley broke into full dance as the choir sang, arms flying, robes raised in full wing like angels.

Out of the corner of my eye, I could see her. Her head thrown back, hair undone, shirt buttons bursting as she threw her chest forward and proceeded to dance. She came out of her shoes as the spirit moved her torso shaking, shimmying across the church. This time, I turned and watched as I pounded those keys. My fingers stroking ivory, my feet pounding wood, my behind rising and riding her shouts of "Yes, oh yes, oh yes…. Thank you. Yes, Father. Oh, Lord, yes." Our voices rang out in unison, "Yes, yes. Oh, Lord, yes…." I played and watched her as she danced and watched me, the smiles in our eyes creeping to the corners of our lips.

That Sunday after service, I was the first one out of the church. And Sister Mavis wasn't far behind. I invited her to dinner. We ate, and talked, and drank a little wine. She told me her story of being a P.K.—preacher's kid—who'd never learned to let herself go till she stepped foot in the Divine Deliverance Tabernacle and felt for herself what she'd witnessed women doing all those years back home in her daddy's tiny church.

I listened to the soft voice that held contrast to the shouts of praise I'd heard earlier. I watched the quiet, almost sacrosanct figure who seemed so small now at dinner, but who loomed large in her worship of her Creator. I listened intently, as she softly spoke about how my music moved her—not just the music itself, but also the idea that a woman such as me, big-framed with large hands, heavy in weight, and so obviously strong, handsome, and masculine, could elicit such spirit from an organ. She stopped and then quietly intoned, "If you could so masterfully do that to an organ, I wonder what you would do to me."

That night, in the quiet of her room, beneath the bristles of the boar's hair brush, I felt the length and weight of her hair cascade down her narrow, athletic back. I kissed the nape of her tiny neck, stroked the slender curve of her shoulders, held the arc of her waist, and watched with envy the tender kiss of her hair as it brushed her naked breast when she removed first her shirt, then mine.

My fingers burned to make music with her, caress the song right out of her throat, draw the breath from her lungs and hear its tonal escape. My hands wanted to pound her keys, hit each right note, bang the inside chords, produce a perfect melody, blend a perfect harmony, strum the perfect beat. I listened for the pitch as my hands moved down her shoulders and along her back, my mouth sprang open, filled with nipples and breasts, and became its own instrumentalist. My hands slid down along her bottom and felt the contracting muscles as she raised her skirt and wrapped her thighs around mine. I pulled her closer.

I felt myself growing as the cotton pressed against my swollen clitoris. Her lips long ago had surrendered to the strength of my loving. I reached down, undid my pants, and let them slide to the floor. I gingerly stepped out of them and my shoes, unzipped the back of her skirt and raised it over her breasts, face, and hair. I carried her into the bedroom.

Miss Mavis Dupree....Mmm Oh yes, what a woman. To say that night she re-created that shout at home with me would be an understatement. Miss Mavis had been wanting for many years to find that sweet release, surrender her body to that good gladness, not just in church, but also at home. In me, Marva L. Malcomb, she finally found the spirit that could set her free.

I lay on the bed and started to speak. Her fingers caressed my lips, as she shook her head, "No." With the flick of a switch on the massive headboard frame of her bed, the room became filled with my music. I listened in awe as the music began to build. I watched Mavis's face. She turned and looked at me, eyes wide open, and softly she smiled. She climbed on top of me and placed my hands on her narrow hips. Bending her knees up, she now squatted over me. Her eyes slowly closed, her fingers tapped the tip of my nipples in time with the music, her glutes kept time on her bottom, her torso began to rock and sway, her head fell back, and her hair tickled the inside of my thighs. "Oh God," the words escaped my lips. "Yes," Mavis replied. Her bottom began sliding across my belly and grinding along my pubic hair. As the music began to grow, so did I. I could feel her edging over me. Lloyd Jr.'s congas seemed to take over in the background and the beat lifted her bouncing along the top of my thighs, the contracting cheek muscles catching and pulling on me.

"Oh God," I moaned.

"Oh yes," she responded.

"Oh God."

"Oh, yes!"

"Oh, God!"

"Oh...yes," our voices cried out in unison.

She bent her knees under and slid the length of her body against mine. I felt her wetness and her hard clit push against my own. The friction between us heated our clits, and wetness streamed between our thighs. Her hair poured over my body, tickling and tantalizing it beyond belief. The choir clapping was ringing in my ears, the bass guitar strummed our heated bodies. We twisted and turned, banged and bonded, arms, fingers, teeth, hair, and juices a mass of motion, gyrating, grinding, pushing, and pumping in time with the music, its crescendo matched by our own.

"Oh God. Yes Father. Oh Jesus. Yes God. Oh God. Yes! Yes! Yes!" Mavis rose as I grabbed her cheeks with both hands. The music continued. We hit the bridge, and Hallelujahs went up everywhere. We could hear the tambourines shaking and the feet stomping.

I pulled Mavis's nether lips to my mouth. Her sigh rose above me when I plunged my tongue deep inside her. Her body shook as I watched her rocking back and forth, struggling against the surrender. Her hands grabbed my shoulders as she tried to wrench away. With each lift, her swollen pussy would void itself of my tongue and then hungrily pound me back into it again and again. She rode this way for several minutes, grabbing my hair and then the headboard, my shoulders, and then the sheets, seeking to find a merciful anchor.

And then it happened. The juices flowing between her thighs slid across my fingers. My thumb edged its way between them and found its way to that last virgin spot and, like an organ key, pushed in and turned on. Mavis rode it, reached around and pushed it further in, pounded my tongue, mouth, and chin with her soft, cavernous pussy. My bottom pounded the bed; my feet pounded the mattress; my fingers keyed her ass; and my lips played an embouchure to her organ. Her shouts reverberated through the night air.

146

As I said, it has been a year since that first Sunday. We've had fifty-one Sundays since. And on every one of them Sister Mavis Dupree re-creates that shout at home with me, Sister Marva L. Malcomb. Gotta go. She's in the bedroom waiting to celebrate our anniversary. And I don't want to keep her waiting. Oh no, no, no. Not Sister Mavis.

Miss Cicero
Dorothy Randall Gray

"There go Miss Cicero, every Saturday, just as regular as you please." The Modeen sisters rocked in their chairs and nodded from the porch as she passed by.

"Yes, indeed. Ain't it sweet how she walk halfway cross town just to read to blind old Mr. Thackeray?"

"Sure is. And she ain't no spring chicken neither. She in her seventies and Mr. Thackeray's older than that! He and her dead husband was tight as tits. Just like family, they was."

"You have a nice day now, hear?" they called out as she tossed a nod their way.

Purple blossomed wisteria vines trailed along the sides of Mr. Thackeray's small white house. The brick pathway bit a swath through the crew-cut lawn, past the figure of a white jockey with a bullet hole in its cap. Miss Cicero held onto the wrought iron railing, and pulled herself up the wide wooden steps.

"Come on in, Miss Cicero," a deep voice called out before she could ring the bell. "My door ain't never closed to you." She locked the door behind her, unpinned the straw hat, and hung it on the hall tree. She stood in the vestibule for a moment, blinded by the darkness of the half-drawn shades, the closed windows, and the smell of fresh roses.

"Pour yourself some lemonade, Miss Cicero. See, I picked you some flowers out my garden?"

"What'd I tell you 'bout using them sharp knives? You done already cut yourself more times than a dog has fleas!"

"I still got all the fingers I need to do what I got to do."

Miss Cicero smiled beside the yellowed keys of the player piano. Slowly, she tipped across the braided rug, coaxed a few petals from the fragrant pink blossoms, and stuffed them into her brassiere.

She pulled striped candies from the cut-crystal bowl, resting her cane against the blue glass table. A pendulum shuttled back and forth behind glass doors of a grandfather clock as it stood guard over sepia photographs of high-collared faces.

"Miss Cicero? You done evaporated or something?"

"I'm fixin' to get the lemonade!"

"Then what you tippin' around the parlor for? I'm blind, but I ain't deaf!"

"Well, maybe you just oughta be. You see too much with those ears. You want something to drink?"

"Liquids is life, ain't they, Miss Cicero? I still got a lot of life left in me, if you know what I mean!"

Her hips pushed the rounded Kelvinator door closed. She drank in the frigid air escaping from the refrigerator, and balanced two glasses of lemonade and a straw bag toward Mr. Thackeray's room.

"I thought you was never coming in here," he said, patting the cushioned rocking chair beside his bed. "Was you meditatin' or something out there? You ain't into that New Age stuff, is you?"

"New Age? Shoot! I'm still trying to deal with old age. Here, take this glass so I can sit down." Mr. Thackeray let the cool lemonade dampen the edge of his mustache. He ran his gnarled fingers along the outside of the tumbler, and brought it to his temples. Tiny violets on a field of white muslin surrounded the silk pajamas he wore over his thin, sturdy frame. His white hair was Fuller-brushed to perfection. He felt Miss Cicero watching his not being her husband.

"Think you gonna live through one more chapter?" she asked as she did every Saturday.

"If the creek don't rise," he answered as always. They sipped in the comfort of an ancient silence.

"By the way, Miss Valdosta sends her regards."

"Well, I hope you didn't bring none of them regards in my house! Ain't that old white biddie dead yet? She got to be 'round a hundred years old by now."

"No, she 'bout your age, I reckon, ninety-four, ninety-five.... Matter of fact, I think she kind of sweet on you, Mr. Thackeray."

"What you talking about, woman? I'm eighty-six, and don't be trying to start no foolishness with me!"

"Didn't I hear something about yo'all fooling around up in her daddy's barn, and you having to jump out the window half-naked when he almost caught you? Heard you was picking straw out your butt for a week!"

"Now, you know ain't a bit of truth to that story, Miss Cicero!" Mr. Thackeray jerked forward, and shook out the pillows behind him. He leaned back against the mahogany headboard, his arms folded under tightened jaws.

Miss Cicero's whole body seemed to chuckle. She pulled the book from her straw bag and began ruffling through its pages.

"And don't think I can't feel you grinnin' at me!"

She could no longer keep laughter from breaking past her lips, bouncing from the mirrored dresser to the fringe on the night table lamp, and landing on the corner of Mr. Thackeray's reluctant smile.

"Woman, why you like to vex me so?" He held his hand out in a question mark, then let it fall to the edge of the bed. "You know I don't be messing with no white meat!" Miss Cicero's finger lightly traced the thick vein on the back of his hand.

"And what kind of meat *do* you like, Mr. Thackeray?" He shifted his body to face her words. She leaned back into the rocking chair and focused on the page. The grandfather clock struck one.

"*'...Janie wanted to ask Hezekiah about Tea Cake, but she was afraid he might misunderstand and think she was interested...'*" she read.

Her voice filled the room's corners and painted his darkness a lighter shade. He lay fully on his side, breathing in the cadence of her words and the lilac persistence of her hair. His vein remembered the touch of her finger and carried his hand across the narrow space between his desire and her chair.

Miss Cicero angled her body toward his outstretched arm and continued to read.

"*'...It was early in the afternoon and she and Hezekiah were alone. She heard somebody humming like they were feeling for pitch and looked toward the door....'*"

Mr. Thackeray found the soft grayness of her hair and stroked each strand as if it were a memory.

"Let it rain, Miss Cicero. Let it rain."

Still reading, she guided his fingers toward the steel restraints holding her twisted bun in place. He removed the hairpins, letting them drop one by one onto the carpeted floor. Her hair, surprised by its sudden freedom, stayed nestled close to her neck.

The gentle toss of Miss Cicero's head caused the wild silver waves to tumble down her back like a waterfall. His hungry fingers walked into the jungle of her hair and massaged her scalp with a spiral strength.

Miss Cicero felt his hand reach inside her for air, and push behind the rise and fall of her chest. She felt him walking the same path her mother had traveled, Cherokee fingers struggling to comb the African presence from her daughter's hair. She sighed and pushed herself from the rocking chair, facing his bed, smoothing the back of her dress with one hand, and holding the book with the other.

"'...The sounds lulled Janie to soft slumber and she woke up with Tea Cake combing her hair and scratching the dandruff from her scalp. It made her more comfortable and drowsy....'"

Mr. Thackeray curled his arm around Miss Cicero's heavy waist. He touched the sight of her face with his fingers, the high terrain of her cheekbones, the clear border surrounding her lips, the warm breath she paused long enough to blow onto his wrist.

She slid her hand inside his silk pajamas, and ran her fingernails up the valley of his spine. The words deepened and lowered her voice. A thin slice of sun slipped past the edge of the shade, casting a shaft of light toward Miss Cicero's making no effort to put the book aside.

He loosened the buttons on her seersucker dress and buried his face in the bouquet of her bosom. His arm moved across the wide expanse of flesh below her waist, pressing a handful of her between his legs.

He kissed the scalloped lace of her black brassiere, moaning and inhaling the sweetness of her loose wrinkled skin. The river rose inside her. She held its waves under tight rein, pushing them back behind the dam. She captured the swell of his body in the hypnotism of her hips swaying from side to side.

"Miss Cicero...." His body trembled.

She played in the coarse hairs at the nape of his neck. His breathing came in staccato exhalations. He squeezed the nipples inside the black fabric, then started to undo its front hooks.

"Oh God...."

Mr. Thackeray pulled the soft dress up around her waist and let his hand glide past the elastic of her satin panties. Miss Cicero clenched her legs like teeth. Her waters beat against the walls of their confinement. The folds of skin floating from her stomach fell into the caress of his fingertips.

He reached into the space between her moist hairs and found it locked. She held onto his hand as he was about to unfasten the last hook. Words still trickled from the book's pages. Bewilderment looked through Mr. Thackeray's eyes. The dampness of his desire swept his pores, and gathered inside his parched throat.

"Goddammit, woman! When you gonna put that book down?"

"I'm waiting 'til I get to my favorite part."

She gripped the fullness of his longing in her hand and read, "*'...She couldn't make him look just like any other man to her. He looked like the love thoughts of women. He could be a bee to a blossom—a pear tree blossom in the spring. He seemed to be crushing scent out of the world with his footsteps. Crushing aromatic herbs with every step he took. Spices hung about him. He was a glance from God....'*"

Miss Cicero set the book on the night table, placing her bifocals on its cover. She kicked off her wide flat shoes and squeezed him again in the warm cup of her palm. As he opened the final hook, an intoxication of breasts, rose petals, and sweat cascaded before him.

She pulled her arms from the unbuttoned dress and let it fall to the floor beside the hairpins. She stepped out of the black satin underwear and stood with her legs open. He lifted her sagging breast and sniffed the fragrant petals that still clung to it. The moist entanglement between her thigh parted to welcome his fingers home.

"Miss Cicero, I'm about to read you *my* favorite parts."

The river's current drew his finger inside her. Again and again it dove beneath the waters, swimming to the surface with muscular strokes, only to plunge deeper into the abyss.

Miss Cicero arched her back and let a slow moan fly toward the ceiling. A tremor ran through her body and dropped into the stockings rolled beneath her knees. She leaned forward to rip open his buttons. His steel passion molded itself to the curve of her hand. She pulled its column to her navel, then pushed it back to its roots.

Mr. Thackeray's groans caught the rhythm of her fingers. He felt for the smell of her breast and drew it into his mouth. With tongue and heart wrapped around her nipple, he sucked fifty years of guilt for having loved his best friend's wife.

"Oh yes! Oh, Jesus, yes!" She dug into the curve of his back.

The dam began to weaken. Pieces of the river spilled over its edge and trickled down Mr. Thackeray's arm. They mingled with perspiration and yearning seeping from his pores, and took him to the place of his dreams. Laughter and screams danced at the back of her throat.

The reins slipped through her hands. She felt the walls being sucked through her skin. They breathed each other into their lungs. He let her breasts fall behind his neck as he lay his cheek on her stomach. He tightened the circle around her hips, and pressed into her with a new fever.

"Let it rain, sweet darlin'. Please, let it rain!"

Laughter and screams leapt to the front of her mouth, and fell into the river, breaking free. The torrent raged through the cracked dam, pulling chunks of concrete, loneliness, and fear of death in its path. Her knees softened. Her bones cried for release. The river rained afterbirth, sweet wine, and buttermilk down her leg.

Mr. Thackeray slowly drew himself from her rainforest,

lightly treading the path toward the tears he left laying on her stomach. He sniffed his wet fingers as if they were roses. Miss Cicero's hand grazed the skin on his chest. Her voice rose from the room, spinning in half-circles.

"Zed," she said, leaning on the rocking chair's edge, "I need to lay down!"

The Call

C. C. Carter

The phone rings. A wet hand picks up the receiver. An acrylic red polished nail attached to a right index finger pushes the TALK button. "Hello?" she answers, winded from toweling off her body.

"What'cha doing?" the familiar deep voice asks, sending shocks down her thigh, causing her to wipe between her legs again.

"I just got outa the shower."

"Damn, that's a lucky bar of soap and how I wish I were that rag. I bet you didn't know that the water was my tongue rinsing off your suds."

She drops the towel, lets it fall on the cold tiled floor, says, "Stop, don't start, I'm going to be late for work."

With receiver wedged between her neck and shoulder, she walks naked toward the bedroom, grabbing feminine hygiene products off the shelf as she passes by the linen closet. "Give me a minute to get situated," she says.

"Not a problem, I'll call you in a few." Click, the phone hums.

The phone rings ten minutes later.

The same red nail presses TALK. "You miss me or something?" Not questioning who's on the other line.

"What'cha doing now?"

"Getting dressed."

"Put me on the speaker."

Four red nails and a thumb take the receiver, place it on the base, index nail presses SPEAKER, she asks, "Can you hear me?"

"So let me guess. Deodorant first, rolling slowly under caramel arms to shaved arches that need my face nuzzled there right now. Lotion oozing in your hand, pressed together between palms then caressing you up arms, between breasts, along indented waist, across stomach. Spreading seductively along hips, adding moisture between ample thighs, slipping slowly toward the back of knees, entering each space of toes— one, two, three, four, swallowing the fifth."

Each movement she dances perfectly with the script, inhaling with word and touch. No longer separated by umbilical cord wires, they merge.

The voice continues, "That baby powder is a lucky mutha 'cause it gets to sink into places, lay there like I wish I could."

She lies down on the bed, on her back, takes the baby powder, tilts it at an angle, and twists the top till the open holes protrude with white specks wishing escape. She closes her eyes and with lacquered red nail tips squeezes the white plastic bottle, releases powder flakes into the air that float over her like stars on clear midnight evenings. They search for a spot, then settle to their resting place in the crevices of her body.

Massages her aches,

"...all over your body, I want to be."

Salve for her heat,

"...where I kiss the spots white powder missed."

Accelerates her breath,

"...my tongue as your washcloth, wiping you clean."

Makes her shake,

"...swallowing toes and fingers while inserting myself into you."

She moans. She trembles. She squeezes wetness dry. She relaxes her thighs. She gets up to wipe off. She puts on fresh lace panties. They tickle.

The voice interrupts, "Baby, you know I'm mad at your bra for getting to palm a hand full of soft flesh. I'm jealous of your panties, smelling your scent all day long. Baby?"

"Yes," she answers weakly from the shutter of the first mini-pulse that vibrates between vulva lips, with more to come.

"Pick up the phone, put it down there, let me kiss her good-bye."

Trembling fingers lift the receiver. With one hand she places the phone down till it brushes the lace of her panties that lightly kisses her hairs. The other hand adjusts the volume until she hears a smack from puckered lips and the words, "Daddy'll see you soon and when we finally meet I promise I'll treat you right and do you good. Now let me speak to your mama."

Hearing this, she brings the receiver to her mouth, listens for the same smack from puckered lips directed toward the ones she speaks with, says, "I'm going to be late, again."

Hears the words, "But how do you feel?"

"Real good."

"Alrighty, then. Have a good day, baby, I'll talk to you tonight."

Eleven P.M. The phone rings once, the second ring interrupted by, "What took you so long?"

"Anticipation is the root of desire. So what'cha wearing?"

She lies and says, "Nothing," so that the voice can keep saying something. All the while removing her underwear as the voice talks.

"Did you think about me today?" in a tone silky-creamy, like sherbet.

"Yes."

"How do I know?"

Propping herself up on one arm, extending the other to run her red nails up and down her thigh, says, " 'Cause I went through four panty shields today and I'm not being visited by my red friend."

A short breath, inhaled before she exhaled words, says, "Oh yeah? Why is that?"

And she starts with the meeting at ten A.M. and the smell of natural herbal deodorant mixing with the scent of Mambo for women, trickling through her blouse as she stood at the easel board, losing her train of thought, 'cause a breeze from the window made her think of a nose once nuzzling there, stopping to lick her lips, remembered that she was not alone in a room with a bed, a phone, and a voice, then smiled at the office full of ten men who watched her do her corporate thang and had them eating out of her hand before they signed on the dotted line for ten mil.

Excusing herself after the closing conquest, rushing to the bathroom. One pad down.

Inhale twice this time, unsteady words, "Damn, ba-by, you, ah, wore, ah, them out."

"I'm not finished," she continued. "My baby powder felt like your breathing on my stomach, whispering in my navel. The lotion that kept my body glowing, left residue of your finger imprints every place you touched me this morning, silky braille words tattooed on my body."

Staccato short breaths, words matching their beat, "That's-it-, ba-by, you- know- what- I- like."

Red nails slip between tight thighs and spread open wet lips, she finishes, "My bra was your two hands cupping my breasts, caressing my thoughts and their softness into erection all day. The cotton middle of my panties perspired, two, then three shields gone, 'cause your tongue brushed softly against my hairs, and your voice echoed secrets in its mouth that only you two knew about. And every time I got up to walk, lips and thighs met 'wishful thinking' yours, 'cause you are so greedy, kissing through the lace, straining to feel finger, touch tongue, know you. Needing to conduct meetings from behind my desk with legs crossed, 'cause standing up made me drip and I only had one shield left in case of an emergency...."

Red fingers push deep inside herself, "wishful thinking" hers, the distance between them narrowing. The voice in her ear vibrates along her neck....

"Yes, Mami, you know what to say, what else?"

"As I drove home, it started to rain. And I was back in the shower with a bar of soap, a rag, and you. Kisses dripping in my hair, on my face, down my back." She hears her own voice purr, "Papi?"

"I'm with you, Mami."

"A sudsy cloth cleansing sensitive neck and erect breasts, once-perfumed stomach, and scented fresh sacred spots."

Deeper plunges, no longer "wishful thinking" hers, red fingers—hers, the voice—hers, the wetness—theirs, together.

"Rain became shower, clothes became towel, soap became tongue and hands, and I could not drive any more. I pulled into somebody else's driveway, pressed the button to let my seat back, shifted the gear to park, pulled my skirt above my hips, spread my legs wide, pushed aside drenched panties and third shield, there would be no fourth, and I let you love me...."

"Say it again, baby," the voice matching her rhythm.

"I let you love me."

In a whispered command, "Say it like you mean it."

"I let you lovvvvvve mmeeee!!"

Their trembles meet at the exhale of moans and heaved breaths.

"Yes, Mami, that's it, I love you."

There are no words, just bodies and escaped sighs separated by wire.

Funky Ride
Janeé Bolden

I'm high when I do it. When I put the CD in the disc player, select track eleven, and then hit REPEAT. Sound hits the ceiling and the floors, floods the walls, this gentle *drip-drop* beat suggesting something illicit and delicious. Outside these windows are urban noises, children playing, bottles breaking, alarms, sirens, ghetto blasters, and hi-fi car stereos. I'm not thinking about what's outside, what's out in that dark dotted by stars, headlights, and streetlamps. What I'm thinking about is inside, is you; is damned fine, dark chocolate and waiting to be pleased by me.

I want to treat you, so slowly I slip between your legs. Undressing you where before I have been too passive. I take a moment to indulge in the sight of you in shorts. You are naked from the waist up, a body that is neither young boy nor man, but something in between. There isn't a hair on your chest. The nipples are chocolate-cherry colored, standing erect, waiting for me to kiss them. I slide my hands over your smooth shoulders and back, so hungry for you that even as I lick one nipple after the other I am making my way back up for your neck. Which is where you begin to dissolve.

See, I'm still fully dressed, and where you've let me take the lead so far, now things are different. You allowed me to move slowly, to let me follow the slow drag—so high, so horny— rhythm of this song. But now I touched your spot, I licked it, I sucked it, and you are open and ready. You don't bother to unbutton my blouse. You yank, you pull, you tear. And even though that blouse cost good money, I'm not mad. I'm turned on. I am wet and you hardly even touched me.

The song keeps reminding me of my initial purpose. I'm here to ride you. You are here to be ridden. My skirt hits the floor, a puddle of fabric at the foot of the bed. My panties follow suit. And then I place my palms flat against your hips, rolling your shorts down, until they get tangled at your ankles. While you are bending over to free your legs I am leaning in to kiss you between your thighs. To the part of you that listens when I say, "I love you." To the part that loves me back.

I close my eyes, find myself soaking in the lyrics, relaxed by the gentle melody, I'm high on this music and eager for sex. *There isn't anything I'd rather be doing, or anywhere I'd rather be,* I think, enjoying the feeling of your penis gliding back and forth past the sensitive part of my lips. This slow stroking of my tongue against your cock, your cock stroking my mouth. My lips, my tongue receiving you and at the same time giving back, all of this is wrapped up in the rhythm of this song, in the rhythm of our bodies. These strokes are foreshadowing the lovemaking that is still to come. I pull forward and back again, daring you, enticing you, raising your excitement another notch. My tongue dancing to this funky lullaby, I open my eyes to watch you. Your eyes are closed and your mouth is open in a small soft *oh*. I brush my fingertips lightly up and down your arms and legs, stimulating the little nerves that I know lie beneath your skin.

You run your hands through my thick, curly hair, stopping

to rub the back of my neck. Then you pull away. It's my turn. You take my hand and we move to the bed.

"Lie down," you command, pointing to the bed. Obediently I lie down, moving my ass closer and closer to the foot until you stop me by grabbing my ankles.

"Right there, baby," you growl. "I gotcha."

"Yes," I whisper, anticipating your touch.

I lean my head back into the mattress, closing my eyes, letting the drunken beat invade my thoughts. The song is nearing its end for the third time, the baritone giving way to a woman's high wails. The words *nocturnal hymn* come to mind. Night holy music. There is something sacred in this moment, in any moment when nothing feels as good as giving someone else as much pleasure as possible. It is the furthest thing from selfish. Giving. Receiving. Giving back again. Now it feels good to be getting. To have your tongue flicking my clit firmly like that little tinkering in the music. A light touch that is anything but delicate. There is tremendous power in your tongue. The song has started over but I am remembering that woman's moans. I am feeling her joy now, the intensity building, the climax approaching. My love comes flooding down, rushing out, just like that song, out against your chin and the sheets. That is the signal.

You can't wait to get inside. All along, that's what we've both been waiting for. The sweetest moment is always just as you begin to enter, when we are both wondering what it's going to feel like. How wet is it. How juicy. And as you sink into my pussy, my walls latch on as tightly as we both can bear. Sugar walls, you call them. And we have a million names for this moment. And a million names for my pussy. That fat rabbit. The golden glove. Jamaica—cuz it's the place you always cum to. And you always like to call it your pussy. To claim it. To declare ownership. You want me to say that my pussy belongs to you, just like I own your dick.

I was high on weed and Cuba libres when all this shit got started. This damned song over and over. And this is my favorite song, just like you are my favorite man, and sex is my favorite moment. And I start thinking tripped-out things while you're up in this pussy. Things like how our fucking is another high. How one moment I'm so wrapped up in my pleasure, in my rapture, and the next moment I'm paranoid that it will all be over way too soon. Thinking how just like with Ecstasy, one minute I'm in hyper-heaven loving all the stimulus in the world and the next I am blissed out on relaxation. It seems a miracle that such a simple motion—in and out, circles along my sugar walls—and each touch makes me feel some sort of joy. Amazing that just as you are touching me, your nerves touch my nerves and they all set each other off. You got me feeling good and I got you feeling the same way.

My love will not dry up on you. This song won't stop until we hit the button, and I will keep on riding until we are both too exhausted to move. And even then, after you've made those funny little noises that you make when you come...after you shudder against me, and I feel your liquid spurt...even after all of that, we still keep on going, relive that sex until we fall asleep. And even when we're sleeping we have dreams about it. Sleeping, I still feel your teeth on my nipple. I still feel the satin-soft feel of your skin against my fingertips. You still feel my pussy clenching on your dick. Our lovemaking is like that.

I like how when we finally decide to stop, you lie on your back, bare-chested, that little bit of moonlight shining on your dark skin, and you watch me walk around the room naked. I like how your eyes follow me as I walk to each of the candles and blow them out. How when I hit the STOP button on the stereo your eyes are still following me, beckoning me back to the bed. Back to you, so that we can roll in balls around each other. So that you can wipe the tiny drops of your sweat from my shoulders.

We sleep with my left hand stroking your soft round ass and your right hand tangled in my curls. We sleep and we dream about all that we've done, and we add and subtract things we forgot to do, or things we shouldn't have done. We're both smiling as we sleep, because we know what will come next when all this dreaming and imagining resurfaces in the next funky ride.

The Warehouse
Jamyla Bennu

Getting settled took up most of my energy that first month I was in New Mexico. I found an inexpensive efficiency in a complex with a pool and spent my first couple of weeks, plus a large sum of my fellowship money, ordering and shipping my supplies. I'd settled into a work-rhythm I liked, but was already outgrowing the capabilities allowed by my limited space.

Any efficiency is "cozy" as a place to live, but when you start including sculptural/photographic installation work in the floor plan, a desert paradise for one moves rather quickly toward "dangerously claustrophobic, oven-hot nightmare." I had to find a studio, and fast. I'd put out a couple of feelers about studio rental: hung posters in cafés, inquired around at the colleges, answered a couple of ads. So far, nothing, but I was trying to be patient.

One morning I came inside after my swim and started making a smoothie for breakfast. While I was blending, I noticed the message light blinking on the answering machine. It figured to be either my mother...or my mother. I'd met no one in my new town yet, and back in civilization exactly two people had my number. One was my sister, and she never called. She'd always understood the importance of solitude to my work. My mother, on the other hand, had been calling two or three times a week to complain about—of all things!—how my latest move was statistically decreasing my chances of Marrying a Good Man or even Meeting Someone Nice. I didn't know which one would be her pet cause today. She alternated.

I pressed the PLAY button, waiting for my mother's wailing. Instead, a polite, somewhat gruff male voice filled my tiny space.

"Hi...this is Marlon Washington, I'm returning your call about the studio rental. The monthly rent is $250 and you'd be sharing the studio with my metalworking shop and a textile artist. I'm actually on the way over there now, if you'd like to come see it. There's no phone in the space, but you're welcome to stop by anytime today at 1546 Water Mill Road.... I should be there until pretty late in the evening. If you can't make it today, feel free to leave a message at my home number and we'll arrange another time."

He left his number and the machine beeped its approval. I stood there for a moment, turning over that voice in my head. It sounded like a brother. Marlon Washington? Of course it was a brother. Even if I didn't get the studio space, it would be great to have connected so soon with another black professional artist. I hoped he was good. Not that I was here to hang out or immerse myself in a "scene," for I had work to do. But I couldn't help hoping that my isolation from an artistic community wouldn't be as painfully total as I'd prepared myself for.

Then my eyes fell to the table-sized stack of clay and wax sculpting supplies that the answering machine was resting on. I snapped to my senses. Meet other artists, my ass—I needed that studio space in the worst way! I nearly stumbled over a bundle of carving implements, I was in such a hurry.

It took me ten minutes to get from shower to door in a strappy sundress, a hold-everything tote bag, and a pair of flip-flops. Desert heat had quickly turned me on to little-bitty dresses. At home I was a strict jeans or overalls girl. But with triple-digit temperatures every day, heat sitting on your skin like a wool hand holding tight, a breezy dress can be your best friend. Plus, I figured there was no harm in showing a little leg to the brother if it would help the real estate decisions move smoothly. I rubbed something sweet-smelling through my short-cropped hair and brushed my eyebrows.

The address was in a fairly empty industrial/warehouse kind of neighborhood. I rang the bell and waited for the hammering to slow down. Then I realized how stupid that was; whoever was hammering probably couldn't hear the bell. I pushed gently with my hand and the door, propped ajar with an ornate metal wedge, swung inward. I headed down a dim hallway and pushed the door at the end.

Wow.

Space just…fell away from my eyes in all directions. From outside, judging by the rows of windows, the warehouse had looked to be a four-story building. Inside, though, it was just one space. The ceiling seemed a mile up, and windows stretched up in many-paned stacks toward the roof. Some of the panes in the front windows had been broken, and there was a loading door open at the back of the building. A breeze ruffled through in a constant, irregular current.

I know because I saw it. It was fluttering through a cascade of cloth. The first third of the huge, high space was hung with enormous sheets of textured, decorated, brightly woven and vibrantly dyed cloth. There were banners, huge ribbons, immense scarves, curling streamers. They were decorated with paint, batik, stitching, dye, stuffing. They spilled down from a scaffolding structure built against the front windows. The light filtered through the colorful mass like a rustling rainbow.

I stayed close to the wall, just taking in the beauty of the spectacle. Then I saw a figure in the middle section of the room, back-lit from the windows and directly across from the doorway in which I stood. He stood over a huge metal-topped table and lifted and swung a pointed hammer, rhythmically. In his other hand, he held a blowtorch trained on his work.

My God, his back. He wore an old green T-shirt, not tight by a long shot but so old and weathered that it stroked every contour of his muscles as he worked. His arms were smooth, and glossy from sweat. A light denim shirt, still tucked into his jeans, hung inside out and down from his waist, as if he'd shrugged out of it in a hurry in the middle of working. The shape of his butt made me want to reach out and grab it. I took a few steps toward him and was pulling out my camera, thinking "no flash, gotta catch the silhouette," before I realized that might be rude. I mean, we hadn't even been properly introduced.

I put the camera back into my bag and called out to him. I said, "Marlon Washington?" first, and then a louder "Hello!" which I had to repeat twice before he shut off the blowtorch. He turned around, lifting a rectangular welder's mask off his face.

My God. His face.

His eyes were so low-lidded they were almost sleepy-looking. A fountain of dreadlocks was tied up securely on the top of his head. His skin was an even bronze-brown, from his clean-shaven cheek to the sweat-glazed back of his hand.

To make it even better, he was walking toward me and starting to smile. His grin widened gradually, slightly sheepish, as he wrestled his way back into his shirt and buttoned it halfway up his T-shirted chest. It was quite a walk from one side of this cavernous place to the other. I figured I could meet him halfway.

My future studio mate—I had already made the claim in my mind—pulled a bandana from his back pocket and wiped his hands before extending one to me. His hand was large, coppery, squared off, rough. I adjusted my bag on my shoulder and we shook.

He was in his middle thirties, I guessed, looking at the threads of gray winding through his thick hair. "Ms. Cooper?" he said, looking directly into my eyes. Not in a flirting way, just straightforward and genuine. And businesslike. Definitely businesslike.

"Yes, but please call me Taya," I said.

"Sure, Taya, thanks. And I'm Marlon. You know, I'm glad you were able to make it so soon. From your message and your name I thought you might be a sister and I wanted to make sure you got first crack at the space. I was planning on answering the rest of the inquiries after lunch." His smile continued its journey across his face to end up lodged securely between two dimples.

Dimples.

He kept watching my eyes but this time with that "don't we got to have each other's back?" kind of pleased-to-meet-you look. I returned it warmly, acknowledging the hookup, holding his hand with both of my own.

"You....rock," I said, a wide grin broadening my own face at the vastness of the understatement. Simple gestures like that can make all the difference for an artist; for anybody. It can be a cold, cold world out there. I looked around me, noting the powerful, organic-looking metal sculpture that surrounded us in Marlon's section of the studio. Above us, an ornate sign festooned with steel vines and hammered-metal blossoms said "EarthWorks MetalShaping" in script so delicately wrought that the light shone through it like music. The entire back third of the place was empty and open. As I watched, it actually seemed to shimmer with potential.

"I need studio space badly," I said, looking back at him. He was watching me with an amused expression in those low-lidded eyes. "But I didn't even dare to dream how perfect this place is. I brought the deposit with me. I'd love to take it. Do you have to approve my work first or something?"

A different kind of warmth spread over Marlon's expression as he glanced down at my hands still holding his. His gaze skimmed down my legs, over my shoulders, to my face. He met my eyes again with an open appreciation.

"I'd love to see your work, Taya, but I'll give you a key right now."

In the next day's early morning cool, I loaded my pickup with my first round of equipment and materials. My mother's keep-yourself-beautiful advice running on unwelcome repeat through my head since adolescence, I rubbed my hands with Vaseline, and put on my work gloves before I started swinging the bags of clay and hoisting the heavy jugs of photographic chemicals.

I thought about my work schedule while I loaded up. I decided I'd still spend the early mornings at home, doing quiet, small-format work such as sketching and claywork. After that, I'd take a swim, have breakfast, take a nap, or spend some various free time. Then I'd pack a little picnic dinner and head to the studio by around two or three. That way, I could get in a good eight or so hours of large-scale work on my installations before it got too late.

My mouth stung, I was so excited.

When I brought my first load to the studio, it was empty. I just got started lifting, rolling, and stacking my truckload of materials in the corner. The whole back of the loft seemed to grow around me, yawning cavernously over equipment that had engulfed my apartment. Compared to the rest of the studio, the space around me looked mighty empty.

I loaded my second truck-full back at the apartment, but it was getting close to ten A.M. and gearing up already for the day's heat. I threw on my bikini and did some laps. After the workout of all that lifting and moving, my muscles really welcomed the smooth, graceful motion of working in the water. I stretched out in the sun and relaxed for about twenty minutes before my excitement got the better of me. I went inside, showered, and packed a big lunch/dinner cooler. Clothes made no more sense today than they had the day before, but it would hardly be appropriate to unload my truck in the nude. I threw on some jean shorts and a tank top and headed out to my new office.

As I pushed through the door wheeling a stack of boxes, Marlon was sprawled out sketching on a blanket spread over his huge work table. When he saw me he jumped up and shouted across the room, offering to help.

"Me and Dolly got it," I said. He looked around behind me for another woman. I pointed to my bright pink hand truck, a sexy pair of eyes painted on her top crossbar. I grinned, "Hey, if you had to lug around as much stuff as I do, you'd develop a pretty close relationship with your hand truck, too."

He laughed, and I told him I'd love some help. As he approached me I grabbed his arm—rock hard under my hand—and pulled him playfully toward the loading door.

We unloaded the pickup companionably. Marlon teased me a little about how strong I was. I've always been built lean and muscular, and after years of building installation environments, and dragging around the artwork that belonged in them, I can pack an amount of weight that surprises most people. I could tell he liked a woman who knew her way around her muscles.

Once the pickup was unloaded, I offered Marlon one of

my juice boxes. They were only half-thawed, just the way I like them. We sat on the loading dock at the back of the warehouse and watched the sky, slurping the slushy sweetness and talking about the desert. Like me, Marlon was originally from the northeast, and both of us had come out west to focus on our work. I told him about my fellowship and he showed me the brochure for EarthWorks, his metal shaping business; which was successful enough to have paid for the old building and still financed his more abstract sculptural work. His portfolio of intricately wrought security gates, bed frames, and ornamental furniture was stunning.

We clicked in that conversation, in a pleasant and familiar way. He wasn't just good to look at: He was open, intelligent, with a great sense of humor. Also, which I respected, his passion for his work was almost palpable.

After our juice break, Marlon got started on a deck railing he was building. I threw myself into The Great Unpacking Project: assembling shelves and organizing my materials. I stacked supplies, connected equipment, hung tools. Used pencil and pad, chalk, and the floor to try to lay out plans for this vast amount of space. Installation and large-scale sculpture projects I'd mused about for years were becoming clearer in concept just from standing in an area large enough to hold them. When I'd finally finished unpacking the first day's loads to my satisfaction, I curled up on my orange corduroy papasan chair and began sketching furiously.

When I looked up next, a blaze of color was crawling down the sky directly outside the loading door. My pickup stood outside, still pulled up to the dock, and Marlon stood in front of me, casting a shadow over my sketchbook. This time there was no denim shirt buttoned demurely over his T-shirt. His chest had the nerve to ripple as he held out an apple in his hand. I took it with a smile, thinking that surely someone had gotten the story backward with that temptation-in-the-garden scenario. Marlon looked even better lit by sunset than he did by daylight or blowtorch. I quickly offered him a turkey sandwich before my aesthetic consideration turned into a full-blown crush on my studio mate. He accepted. Dragged over some snackables and a chair.

We munched and talked for hours while night descended, soft. He made jokes, talked about the town, and even flirted with me a little. I was warming to him like cornbread rising.

I asked about the other artist in the space, an MFA student who he told me used the studio most during the wee hours of the morning. "Cassie's very talented, very industrious. She's been here for a year. I don't see her often, though. We keep different schedules."

Marlon pulled two dark, plastic-wrapped squares from a brown paper bag.

"We do have one studio arrangement you should know about: I leave weed in the table drawer, and she leaves brownies." He stretched his hand out to me, offering. "They take about an hour or more to kick in, but after that you're good for a long while. Eat one now, you'll go to sleep smiling."

He winked and I laughed, unwrapping my square. Once again, I couldn't have dreamt it more perfectly. I thanked him, and sank my teeth into the richest brownie I'd ever tasted. It was like an injection of solid chocolate in my jugular vein. I couldn't even taste the herb. I ate the whole thing in three bites and finished almost breathless, licking my fingers ravenously and fumbling for my bottle of water.

Marlon was licking his own fingers and laughing at me.

"I was the same way the first time I had Cassie's brownies. They were so good I ate three of them before I could stop. I was high for two and a half days. I've since learned one is enough."

He picked up the brown bag and our empty drink boxes and pointed out where the brownies were kept. "You're welcome to them," he said. "Anytime."

He squeezed the top of my shoulder and crossed behind me, heading for the kitchen. His casual stroke was firm and warm and reached so far down into my weary muscles, I almost moaned. He stopped behind me and kept his hand in place, carelessly working my clenched flesh and reducing me to a babbling idiot.

"Damn, woman. You've really been working, huh?"

My head did something affirmative from where it was lolling over one shoulder. His touch felt good. Beyond just "the-man-is-fine" good. I mean, really good.

"You want me to rub your shoulders down?"

I nodded again. Got my eyebrows into the act and asked a wordless question. Something like, "How are you doing this to me," but more professionally phrased.

"I did a massage therapy certificate soon after I moved out here," he said, squaring off behind me and grasping my shoulder joints in his hands like ben wa balls. "Four years ago, now, I guess. Right after my divorce."

His hands were working light and magic into my spine. I sat up straight in the papasan chair and slowly leaned forward as his hands worked their way to my lower back. *Did he say divorced?* asked my mother's voice in my head. *You're almost thirty-three, Taya. Remember the last time you—*

I did remember the last time. I'd come out here partly to be as far away from Mr. Last Time as humanly possible. I forced my mind back from where it was racing. Marlon was a trained professional, I thought sternly at myself. He sees a cramped muscle; it's his job to ease it. And you, Little Miss Chocolate Orgasm, are here to work.

After five heavenly minutes, Marlon had kneaded my back into a pliant pulp. I was so well-wrung that I whimpered a little when he stopped.

"I'll finish that job up for real when you're done moving," he said, standing up again and picking up his stuff. "You'll feel like a million dollars."

"Well, I already feel like half a million," I muttered into the pillow. "I might have to make change after next time."

He laughed and walked toward the kitchen with our trash. I just lay there, breathing deeply. Trying to keep my thoughts chaste.

Brownies always hit me late. When I went home that night I loaded the last of my materials into the pickup, trying to wait it out. In the end my exhaustion won and I went to sleep thinking I'd missed my high. Not so. The early morning sun streamed into the room with a liquid sweetness that meant the glory had arrived. I rolled over onto my sketchbook and was scribbling wildly, trying to hold onto the ends of my dream and catch up to the day's ideas already plunging around in my head. I read a little, cracked up watching Rikki Lake, wrote my sister an e-mail. I sat on the balcony in the deepening heat eating cold pineapple chunks from the fridge. Then I rinsed the sticky juice off my forearms and dove into the pool.

Swimming was a glorious dance of water and human molecules, but I didn't swim long. I couldn't wait to go to work! This time, it was not only the heat that influenced my choice of dress. A slew of not-so-innocent thoughts about Marlon whirling through my head, I put on the merest Indian cotton halter, a similarly scant denim skirt, and some sneakers. Vanilla body spray, just because. Threw work gloves and Vaseline into my bag and jumped into the truck.

I really wanted to get the rest of my stuff unloaded early. After yesterday it was clear Marlon wasn't the kind of man to let me lift alone, and I felt kind of bad about disrupting his process. I moved around the new space like a dynamo in the morning's deepening heat, working to finish fast.

I was wheeling Dolly, empty, back out to my truck when Marlon's battered blue Cherokee pulled up. He jumped out in an orange T-shirt and khakis, resplendent in the sunlight. Hair tied back tightly in a piece of leather and hanging down to his waist. He shaded his eyes with his hand.

"Hey, Taya. Heading out or coming in?"

"Neither," I said. "I just finished with the last load of stuff from my apartment. I'm taking Dolly back to the truck and then I'm here for the day."

He smiled.

"...So you're finished moving?"

I nodded my head, pure joy leaking out of the corners of my grin.

Marlon stepped to me and spun me right around, gripping my shoulders and upper arms with those amazing hands.

"Well, then, we've got one celebratory welcome massage due in full, don't we?"

Dolly stood abandoned in the drive but I was in no condition to move her, having already melted.

Marlon spread the bright Mexican blanket over his metal-topped work table and topped it with the big round cushion from my chair. With great ceremony he arranged me face down on it and the miracle began.

He slathered his hands with a cooling peppermint lotion and started on my bare upper back. His fingers were dancing between my muscles, squeezing life into every pore of my skin, deftly untying the back of my halter to stroke down either side of my spine.

His hands skirted down the outside of my hips and worked the soothing lotion from the backs of my thighs, over the curves of my calves, to the arches of my feet. I chewed on my lip to keep my vocalizations to a minimum, but nothing could completely stop the sighs and occasional groans as he manipulated every fiber of my body.

My muscles were whirling under the surface of my skin. He chased three days of accumulated work-weariness down each limb and out my fingers, my toes. Pushed strain out from my lower back and up along my ribs. He squeezed and stroked the palms of my hands, the bottoms of my feet, the nape of my neck, my lower back. I fell spinning into a pool of peppermint light.

I thought I felt the air of a soft laugh against the back my neck. I thought I felt him kiss me, very lightly, behind my ear. But I was asleep five seconds later. So I might have been dreaming.

I didn't sleep long. About fifteen minutes, Marlon told me when I awoke with a start. I was sprawled out belly down on the cushion and he was sitting cross-legged on the table an arm's length away from me, acting like he was resuming a conversation with a participating individual instead of with me, a dazed, catnapped woman just blinking into embarrassed consciousness.

"It's a great compliment when someone falls asleep after a session," he continued. "To me, it means I've relaxed you greatly."

"You can say that again," I said, moving my body around experimentally. "I feel like I should have some new magical power, or be glowing or something."

"Who says you're not?" he asked. His eyes swept down me. I crossed my legs a little and perched my chin in my hand. Watched a sliver of colored light slip between the rustling fabric at the windows, slide up Marlon's arm, over his shoulder, and away. "You are very beautiful, Taya," he said. "I took the liberty of watching you while you slept, I hope you don't mind."

Under other conditions, I might have blushed, or thought about changing the subject. Instead, I smiled. Laid my head back down on the big round cushion and made a confession of my own.

"I think it's kind of sweet. Plus, I have a confession to make, anyway: I watched you while you worked that first day I came to see the place. Almost took a picture, I couldn't help it. Even your back is beautiful."

I reached out lazily and briefly interlaced my fingers with his. Brushed the roughened surface of his palm with my thumb, ran my small, square fingers in and out of his larger, squarer ones. I turned it over and traced the veins on the back of his hand and asked about a small scar there. For a number of minutes, we talked across arm's distance, squashed flat by the midday heat and all my muscles feeling like rubber bands. Electricity crackled between us, almost visible, running up our arms like lightning.

"What's the name of that fellowship you're on, Taya? The Ford?"

"The Newcombe," I said. "They call the program the Roaming Residency."

"And you could've gone anywhere you wanted?"

I nodded. His hands were moving up my forearm now, chasing the electricity up past my elbow. I watched in pure wonderment as he worked his way up to my shoulder.

"What made you choose Taos? So far away from everyone you know?"

His face. His chest. His sleepy-looking eyes. His dancing, twisting metal work. I kept watching his hands on the skin of my arm. Little shocks shook my flesh.

"I don't know," I said. "I guess I just wanted to be alone."

I sensed the little smile before I even saw it play across his face. I looked up, saw the dimple; it was gone; there it was again.

"Yeah," he said. "Me too."

Marlon raised my hand to his mouth and kissed the palm, softly, squarely in its center. His lips parted and the tip of his tongue darted out, painting delight down my lifeline. He bared his teeth and bit succulently at the flesh padding the base of my fingers, ran his tongue briefly between each joint, watching my face with open eyes. I never knew my hand could make me feel so good.

I think I breathed that last out loud.

To prove that my hand could feel even better, he slipped two of my fingers joint-deep into his mouth and I lost all will to breathe. Surprising myself, I accomplished my most superhuman feat of strength ever: I wrenched enough energy together to untie my halter with my free hand. Spent, I rolled over and looked up at Marlon, framed in rainbow light and kneeling above me with a look of smiling anticipation.

I had already surrendered my body to this man and with oil and pressure he'd put me to sleep. Now, with tingling electric touch he was waking me up. His hands were suddenly everywhere, chasing little jolts of awareness down my back, up my stomach, behind my knees, over my nipples, between my thighs. I hardly knew where to focus my attention, I felt so surrounded by him. I couldn't move a muscle except in reaction to his touch—which means I was thrashing all over the cushion.

And he was only just beginning. Marlon kneeled between my thighs, and ran his finger down the front of my cotton thong, hovering over the moist heat at my center. He sucked my middle and ring fingers back into his mouth, biting their tips, scraping rough, hard licks down their fronts, planting wet slurps at the base. One of his fingers dove under the elastic between my thighs and painted swirls around my clit. He plunged his finger into my pussy and, at the same time, scissored hard between my fingers with his tongue.

I had no bones in my body.

My underwear was gone. My thighs were rubber, wide open and trembling worthlessly for all their much-admired latent muscle power. I coalesced, became a point of dense liquid swirling around his hands. He curved his finger upward, pushed slowly in and out of me, my walls yielding juicily to its calloused grain.

He let my hand out of his mouth and folded over me, hungry, chewing, sucking on one of my nipples and pinching the other. My fingers felt so abandoned that I thrust them into his hair: rough and warm on the top of his head; wiry, soft, and hot near his scalp. I untied his leather cord and a thousand tickling tentacles fell forward onto my breasts, shoulders, throat, smelling like frankincense where they fell onto my face. I writhed, gasping, as his hair cascaded around me, changing the light into a rough and shadowed thing. He slid another finger into me alongside the first.

I got my muscles to move.

Some of them, anyway. Legs were still worthless, splayed wide and quaking around Marlon's diving fingers, but control of my hands was returning. I unbuckled the belt of his jeans in a hurry, opened the button, lowered the zipper. He raised his kissing, nibbling head from my rib cage and kissed me, seriously kissed me, while I coaxed his heavy dick out of his clothes with both hands.

His cock fell free into my palms and I could tell that it was sweet. Didn't even have to sneak a look. I dove my tongue around his mouth and stroked his rigid length with both my hands. When I ran my thumb up over the head I slid into a pearl of slickness. My favorite. I brought my thumb into my mouth to taste him while I smoothed my other hand over the slippery head of his dick. A tremor went through his body, starting at his hips and ending when he dropped his head back into our kiss.

Sucking on his tongue, I placed the head of his cock at my entrance. The first of its inches pressed in easily. He stayed there a moment, a solid surprise, then gripped my shoulders and drove deeper, steady, rocking, carving himself in gradually and resting only when the base of his pelvis pressed against mine. I wanted to say something—"Bravo!" "Pleased to meet you!" "Thank you, sir, may I have another?" …Something. But my mind was completely blank for the moment. Marlon hung over me with a pleased, slightly expectant expression, looking like he was about to do a push-up. We stared at each other inside the curtain of his hair.

Then we laughed. He moved down onto his elbows and I clenched my vaginal muscles around the heat of his dick, and didn't have to say anything.

He started to push in and out of me, slowly. "Rock-hard" meant something different now that I'd felt him inside. He slid out repeatedly, keeping just his head between my lips and then running his solid length back up into me. Each time our pelvises met, my pussy got happier, taking his size with growing enthusiasm, gobbling his dick completely. Succulent noises squelched between us.

Marlon's hand reached down and cupped my ass, lifted one leg up toward his shoulder. He stroked inside me so deep it made my eyes cross. His face was inches from mine but I couldn't see him. I gnashed my teeth together and bit on the ends of his locks, clawed my neat, filed nails across his magnificent back, tried to drag him deeper inside me. He scooped me up, pulled my torso inches off the table where I hovered, sustained by and centered on his plowing dick, supported by his iron arms.

I was nothing but an orgasm, shrieking and moaning. My arms were spread open, flung wide on the table's blanketed surface. I rode my wild climax, bucking. I was still coming when Marlon put me down on the cushion with my hips at its edge and slammed his cock forcefully from an inviting new angle. I swung my legs upward and held them at the ankles, giving him an eyeful of his dick plunging in and out. No man I'd ever been with hadn't liked to watch, and I was fucking a man I'd just met in our shared place of business. I figured, why go halfway with it? I wrapped two fingers around the base of his cock and massaged my engorged clit with my thumb.

Marlon clutched my hips and started twisting his waist, churning into me and, unbelievably, growing even stiffer. I wrung the last of my climax off on his magnificent dick.

With my pussy still clenching from my peak, I swung upward, sliding off Marlon's ready shaft and wrapping my lips around it before he could say anything. I sank that thick thing as far into my throat as it would go and folded my hands around the rest. I drank the taste of my pussy from his flesh and milked it with my tongue, lips, fingers. Marlon put his hand on the back of my head, not rough but insistent, and I fucked my mouth up and down on him until I felt that jerk/pulse/quiver that meant he was coming.

I stroked his cock firmly and kissed the very tip, whirling my tongue around the head and keeping my lips parted. I let him see it shoot into my mouth a little before I dove down onto him, feeling his cum splash warm down my throat. His hands dug into my shoulders and back as I drank his juices down—not at all like a trained masseuse.

That time, we both fell asleep.

Palimpsest

R. Erica Doyle

You are a third-generation beast in a first-generation world of open legs. You were six when you read your mother's Marquis de Sade. It explained so much about things in the house. Kama Sutra at seven, but you remained unimpressed. Likewise, at eight, by the flaccid illustrations in *The Joy of Sex*. However, the paintings of Shoji at nine—the kimonos parted over thick white penises, the arc of them shining into pleated vulvas—excited you.

You fuck artfully, are disappointed by graceless fumblings. You give them one more chance, just to placate your horrified friends. To say, I fucked her twice, avoid the one-night-stand hisses. Not that the PR helps your reputation or your sex life. Some things do not improve with time.

You talk to them first, pay close attention to details, are interested and easily amused. Women like that. Always a voracious reader, you turn their pages, memorize the deep structure of their grammar, their adjectival clauses. A question in private that puts them off guard. Women are so polite. So crisscrossed with borders. Sometimes it's like stealing. Taking something you don't really want just to. Get away with it. Sometimes you tell them you love them. Sometimes, not often, this is true.

You hold back enough to keep them curious. Women like that. You are wounded enough to be salvageable. Women like that too—fixing things. Taking in the broken wing you drag like a decoy.

You are hungry. Each one tastes different. You lavish your tongue wherever they push your mouth. Creases slick with sweat and hair and the particular liquid of an armpit. You are not clean. You are not fresh. You are not pleased with extended foreplay. You want the fuck. Your hands as full of cunt as the stretch can dare, the edge of pain and fear. Their screams delicious bells pealing, their small large rough soft hands grabbing. Sometimes you make an offering of yourself. They think they take and you open wide to swallow them whole.

You are not generous.

One holds herself away from you and fucks your cunt dry with the thick black cock, sweat rain, and, unrelenting, fucks your ass, then slathers the lube and turns you over again and again.

One pushes your fist away. You rewind and tease her clit until she begs for it, kneels ass moon full. A difficult position, but you oblige, blood spilling from your wrist and aching fingers.

One stumbles in the shower against your soap-slick arm, gasps choking on the water full in a mouth turned away from you, a tongue you sucked on for hours. A shining slap and push through to the cervix soft circle.

One you coax and beg and cajole. She doesn't say yes but she doesn't say no. You suck her asshole until her cunt is wet and fuck her with your tongue until she sighs.

You do not make promises. You do not plan to keep. You are not conjunctive.

One sits on your cock while you think about her boyfriend.

You are perfect.

One cries from her urethra while you suck her clit.

You are dangerous.

One's anus spirals out around your finger.

You are unapologetic.

One's youth gives beneath your knee, crisp indentations.

You are born.

When you can't fuck, hunger makes you walk the streets alone and weep. If the moon is full your womb is an aching crater. The doctor says your hormones are fucked up. She wants you to take pills to stabilize them. They make you feel pregnant and bitter and you won't stop smoking. You quit taking them, though it means you will get cancer. The eggs struggle against the membrane and wait to be let out, die, and decay there, festering cysts. On the sonogram, your ovaries look like asteroids against the tulips of your fallopian tubes.

When you can't fuck, you write about not fucking. You plan the next escapade, have dreams where you hook up with blue-eyed Australian men. You kiss women young enough to be your daughters, masturbate several times a day, and get no work done. Your friends say that this is good for you, that you need to stop fucking so much. That if you do it less you will think about it less. They are lying, as usual. You think they are jealous of how you feed, how they repress their own gluttony. You think of sins, of church, of priests, of how the hood of the clitoris is like the nave of a cathedral.

You are not penitent.

When you haven't fucked for long enough, you make bad fuck judgments.

You fuck a lawyer who has never fucked a woman before. "Women are so kind," says the virgin. "Women are sensitive and caring." Her hope is a virus. You say nothing. She makes good rum cake and wants to watch TV. You fuck her tiny cunt with three fingers while you patiently suck her clit. You are unceremonious. You disabuse.

You fuck an insipid poet who is too fat for your taste. She sends you poems you claim were never received. She calls the night you are fucking the lawyer. You tell her—I am fucking the lawyer, we'll talk tomorrow—and turn off the ringer. Let the answering machine take her eighteen pleas.

You fuck your best friend the night before your father's funeral.

You fuck your ex's best friend the week before you get back together with your ex.

You fall in love.

You fall in love with a star in a different constellation, city, state, relationship. Her lovers have good credit and dark hair. She meets you in the back room of your cunt, in the crevices you left unturned. You fuck her in the armchair before the fireplace when her lover is away, pull down the laces of her mouth, and shove your hand into the bruised cuff of her cunt. Her face is a quick flush of heat, lips purple from your teeth. You blind, bind, beat. Her geography wears at your nipples. You map her in reticent bodies, know a crystal glass by how it sings beneath your moistened fingers.

When you are not fucking, your generosity knows no bounds. When you have no more money, you share your food. When you have no more food, you give good advice. Everyone tells you, you should be a therapist.

You have been lying since you were six. The Marquis de Sade was all about presentation. Your origin is a story your mother used to quell the troops. Your luteinizing hormone will not release the eggs. Cunt judgment. The gynecologist laughed. You were eighteen years old and she thought your dickless state was a joke. You are not a joke and you have your own dicks. You refuse to make love. Take the consumptive tunnel and give it a fuck. The edge of the tub, the arm of the sofa, your brother's rocking horse, fruit, vegetables, tongues, fists, nipples, fingers, toes, toothbrushes, bottles, candles, handles, plastic, porcelain, silicone, glass.

You are not injured. You are not healing.

You are taking it lying down.

Notes to You
Michele Elliott

day one:

girl,

    first day here. flight was manageable. these accommodations are far superior to the last conference. just getting settled from the airport. gazing out the window over the lake. thought about those scars on your body. the scars on your neck. imagined kissing them. pressing my lips against that raised mark.

    you like me to mark you. you enjoy the marking as play. the making is even more exquisite. I wonder how you got those other marks. (you linger in the safety of your secrets.) and I wonder what it would be like to let go and cherish those marks. (those not made by me.) permanent. to kiss them. maybe the one on your neck. really kiss it. kiss the one beneath it. pull you close and tight. give and know the giving is received, without hesitation. no questions. simply become that cherished moment. become the one cherished. would you give yourself to me?

    6 days until I see you again.

day two:

shhhh.

in my bed, kitten. the hot summer air surrounding us. after a long day of workshops I imagine you here. gently licking my mosquito bites. massaging my tired limbs until I force you to stop. I feel desire in your hands. smooth and press it into my flesh like expensive oils. I know that you can't not touch me. if I said *no,* would you seal your desire from me? or give it to me, knowing it's your desire that feeds my endless hunger?

show me your desire. submit in honesty. like a kitten pulled by the scruff of the neck, you go limp with desire just to see me smile. will you focus on minutia if it pleases me? wait all day in one place if I ask it of you?

5 more days until I see you again.

day three:

let's revisit one of the nights before I left.

I called you late and you came over immediately. hitchhiked from the outskirts of the city just to get to me. barely inside the door I had you tell me of your travels and then strip down in silence. fold your clothes neatly in a pile on the floor while I watched. it was lovely, knowing what you did to get to me. I could smell the excitement on your skin. I made you sit in the middle of the floor, bare ass on cool, hard wood. you squirmed and I frowned at you. so shy and unsure, brown skin blistering under my gaze. and still I made you wait, because it was delicious.

eventually I had you sit on the low stool. the one I had refinished just days before. I told you that you would be breaking it in. ass on the edge, knees bent and open. I told you some of the nasty things I could do to you. and we both watched your wetness form, grow strings heavy with gravity, fall and collect itself in tiny pools on the floor...

4 more days...

day four:

later, I had you crawl on all fours, ass in the air, inviting.

I knew what you wanted. needed. but I had worked you over so hard the day before. I wanted to be sure you were sure. you're still so new to this. so I drew you a bath with fragrant oils. let you soak away the muscle cramps and strains. gave you a glass of wine and washed your body slowly. lingered over the fresh bruises that made you so proud. I took pleasure in your joy and accomplishment for having me mark you. display ownership. spoil. pamper.

your body a glistening mixture of water and oils, I had you crawl back over to the stool. back to the same spot you inhabited earlier, only this time I sat on the stool, legs spread wide. I beckoned you forward to the spot I had marked off with masking tape before your bath. back to the little pool of your wetness cooling in the night air. you sniffed it so lovingly, ass high in the air on display. I had you lie flat. and then slowly, exactly as I instructed, you gently lapped up your sweet treasure.

couldn't get enough. I had you get in my bed for the first time. you rolled your body around on my sheets. I demanded that you come for me while I watched. then I dressed your naked flesh in my overcoat. tucked your hungry body into a cab. into the early morning light. sent you home to think. to remember.

3 more days.

day five:

it's been a very long day.

events went well into the evening and I find myself a little tired. I think about your tongue, kitten. how eager and persistent it is. so willing. inviting. your pussy is not always so open. sometimes you hold back from me. is it fear? is it too much for you? or too little? where is your heart, little one? do you protect it from me? bundle it off somewhere like winter coats in mothballs? it's always summer with me, if you are warm and willing. if you show me your promise. submit in spirit and posture. shut out the world, little one. hush. I can give you what you desire.

2 more days.

day six:

your message said that I already have you.

that you feel greedy, hungry for the chaos created by my touch, my belt, my bite. you said that you can hide nothing, deny me no thing. that your heart feels safe. and that you are afraid and shy and confused. I need to be sure that you are sure. this is not just a game. it is everything. I want all of that wild spirit you keep trying to hide. when you are helpless is when you are the most powerful. this is the moment I want. everything. upturned and vulnerable tearing back into me, demanding more. hungry you to match insatiable me.

that first day I took you. at the party. in the basement. we'd only been dating. barely. I took you in the basement. you had a little to drink, were talking a lot of trash. and I could only smile. I took you in the basement. ripped down your pants. bent you over the table, worked you over hard with the flat end of a big scrub brush. while everyone else was upstairs—unaware—you screamed and cried out. you struggled, confused and excited. you didn't care who heard you beg me for more while I pulled your hair and made you say it. you didn't care who heard you wail and open up. and when I let you go and you slumped down to your knees—and spontaneously thanked me—I caught a glimpse of you. a mirror reflecting desire. yes. I need to be sure you are sure.

1 more day.

day seven:

I am packing to come home now.

you'll accept this message from my hand. I dreamt of you last night. dreamt of dressing you. selecting your clothes. watching you slip them onto your body. I play with you along the way. tease you. work you up and make you wet. I take you out to a restaurant where I meet some of my friends. me laughing with them. you quiet. docile. you sitting at my feet. my friends disturbed, anxious about your submission. when they ask you what you get from all this you answer simply, *she is my reward. that is everything. that is enough.*

you as my girl. my kitten. doing whatever I ask. seeking always to please me. speaking only when spoken to. looking to me first. using your eyes to ask my permission to do anything. I know what you need. look to me now. eyes downcast. service. my pleasure your only concern. obedience the meat you cut your teeth on. desire an insatiable balm. you are bound to me. broken by me. set free.

Meeting Eros
Carol Smith Passariello

Photographer is a term Rosanna interchanges readily with *professional voyeur* in describing her work. She invites the public into private moments through the lens. Her latest exhibit at the SoHo Blaze is titled "Everyday Eros." From the looks of the crowd, she is finally getting long-overdue recognition from the New York arts community. Critic types, agents, and press are crawling all over the room.

When I'm finished people-watching, I turn to the amazing photos lining the whitewashed walls. In the images are extreme close-ups capturing the facial expressions of people going about their daily lives, experiencing the world through their senses: a woman caught up in the delight of sucking the sweet juice from a ripe papaya, an old man inhaling the yeasty aroma of freshly baked bread, a child listening to the magical sound of the sea in shells.

My favorite collection of Rosanna's is "Mother's Milk" where she features nursing mothers and their babies in different stages of disrobing, feeding, and enrobing. But I think her most meaningful work is the collection of self-portraits she did after her mastectomy, reconstruction, and subsequent deconstruction, called "My Breasts, My Self." In some of the shots she is pale, breast-less, bald, and rail-thin from chemotherapy, but she still recorded her journey through cancer for the world to see.

True artists are so generous with the truth, and that opens them to high praise and low blows. They are also painfully and pleasurably aware, which often leads them to live between states of elation and periods of deep depression. Rosanna turns every traumatic loss into an opportunity to tell a story. She also turns careless glances into meaningful images. Any way you slice it, the sister's main motivation is to bring life into focus.

I could never bare my breasts for the camera now, but I posed for Rosanna with my newborn daughter ten years ago. I had some lovely titties back in those days. I gave the best of my tits to my daughter, who is now the proud owner of prepubescent buds. Thank God tight tits aren't a prerequisite for sexy. Shit, I put a good bra on and never miss a beat. Everything else is still standing at attention, and while I may be rounder than some, after a couple of kids, one must be thankful to still be in the game. The third party of our trio, Chloe, could still pull it off. Even after breastfeeding twins, she has the perky tits of a fully blossomed teenager. God bless her.

Rosanna used us as her subjects in another one of her projects—a series of shots called "Play Group" where we are shown playing with each other and our children: see-saw, hula-hoop, hide and go seek, tag, doctor, Marco Polo. Rosanna showed us how young and sexy we look when we smile and romp with abandon. Playfulness is the fount of youth, and apparently it is also the prelude to fantastic sex.

I met Rodney seven years ago through our mutual friendship with Rosanna and Hampton. Rodney had gone to school with Hampton, married another classmate, and moved to the West Coast. When I met him, he was in the middle of divorcing her and had moved into Hampton and Rosanna's suburban hideaway temporarily while he looked for a place in the city. They set us up on a blind date to double with them on a weekend in Martha's Vineyard, and we've been inseparable ever since. I swear that man had to have been starved for both sex and food for his entire marriage. Apparently food and sex were one and the same enemy, not to be overindulged or taken lightly. He's getting plenty of good eating now, literally and figuratively. I don't know how a marriage is supposed to survive without good food and good sex. Shit, it's hard enough to recommit to the daily grind. To do so while still in search of satisfaction would seem nearly impossible.

Tonight we're gathering at Rosanna and Hampton's house for an "after party" celebrating the opening of Rosanna's exhibit. We don't really need a reason to party, but we party harder whenever we have a legitimate excuse. Everybody's kids are back at our house, where we have Rosanna and Hampton's oldest daughter, Sydney, in charge for a small fee and a pizza delivery.

When he opens the door Hampton's hair is an ocean of relentless waves, tumbling away from his forehead, carelessly revealing a sinister widow's peak. Everything beautiful about the male anatomy follows that downward-pointing arrow: his intense eyes, then his generous lips and neck and shoulders and chest and back and forearms and horn-playing fingers. But he's off limits because we're both married to mutual friends. I know he's attracted to me too, but as I tell my husband all the time, I am merely reacting to what I can see but can't touch, to what I can smell but can't taste. Other men are just like food to me. Good to look at, great to smell, and hard to resist.

After a few dirty martinis, champagne toasts, and polite conversation, most of the fifty or so people in the room start their good-bye hugs and kisses. The few who hang around start up clandestine conversations about one another, cloaked as critical analysis of the laws of attraction and the true nature of mating in the animal kingdom. When we notice all the men in the room staring at the only single woman left at the party—Chloe—Rosanna and I come to the conclusion that we are witnessing the results of our own big mouths. Women do most of the work for other women by telling their husbands and boyfriends all about the sexual escapades of their friends, thinking they'll be turned off by promiscuous behavior. The only thing those men get from those conversations is hot on the trail of some got-to-be-good pussy with plenty of practice. I don't talk to my husband about my women friends unless I want him fantasizing about them while he's fucking me.

Chloe is a freelance journalist. She's always good for starting some shit on the scene with her loaded, open-ended questions that she calls "critical queries." When the party has boiled down to the usual suspects—Rodney and I, Hampton and Rosanna, and Chloe and Sam—she introduces a game where you pull a name from a hat and as graphically as possible describe the person's most attractive qualities: an intellectual version of spin-the-bottle. The trick is, if you get someone you simply don't find attractive, you can pull one more name, but that's it. And once you've chosen, you have to keep your eyes closed so that people won't catch on from your eyes focusing in on the subject of your description. We start in a circle and pass the basket counterclockwise.

Chloe pulls first. "I pulled a woman, but let me see. Her hands are delicate massage masters, goose bump raisers, tantalizing teasers like tiny feathers all over the back of your neck."

Rosanna and I smile at one another, simultaneously raise our hands, and begin to wriggle our fingers seductively in the air like exotic dancers.

Hampton fishes around in the basket and pulls next. "I

pulled a woman too, and thank God because I'm not trying to describe what's sexy about a man." He closes his eyes. "OK, she smells good. Like the way an open flower leaves an invisible map for bees. It just draws you in and you want to find out where all that sweetness is coming from."

Then it's my turn. I am afraid everyone will know exactly whom I am describing, so I hold back. "He's the kind of man who clearly loves his wife but won't take his eyes off of you until he knows you get the message that you're absolutely beautiful to him."

"That was weak," Rosanna says.

"Yeah, girl. Now you *know* you can do better than that, Meena. Come on," Chloe says.

"OK. You asked for it," I say and close my eyes again. "His hands are basketball palming, waist holding, ass squeezing, take-your-breath-away big." When I open my eyes, all the men are looking at their hands and stretching their fingers to make their hands look bigger. "I knew y'all were going to do that," I say and pass the basket.

Rodney pulls twice. I am tuned into every syllable. "I never thought about hitting it for real because all hell would break loose, but the thought of it is enough to make me wonder how soft her lips might really be and if kissing them would be considered grounds for divorce. She's the kind of woman who makes you have to fight yourself not to get hard in the middle of a crowded room because when she talks to you all you can imagine are those juicy lips wrapped around your dick."

"Oh, shit," Hampton jumps up to give Rodney a high five.

"Well, it seems like the brothas are getting the hang of this game mighty quickly," Rosanna says.

"Shit, I just hope one of them is talking about me," I add with a laugh.

"Me too," says Chloe.

Then Sam pulls. He is looking straight at Rosanna. "Every

time she kisses me hello she puts her arms around my neck and pulls me in just close enough to know how easy it would be to swoop her up and wrap her big, pretty legs around my waist."

"You're supposed to close your eyes, Sam," Rosanna says.

Then Rosanna pulls and closes her eyes. "Whenever he speaks to me, he looks me straight in the eyes. I like that he is not afraid to really see me. I like that he seems to enjoy what he finds when we are eye-to-eye."

"Well, that's everybody. Do we want another round?" Chloe asks. Everyone is digging the feeling and she gets a unanimous yes. We pass the last of the champagne for refills. Only this time no one is waiting for the basket.

"When he pours me a glass of champagne he makes sure the bottle is far enough away so the bubbling liquid splashes around the sides of the flute and creates a miniature tidal wave. I love that because even after I catch the overspill in my mouth, there are a few droplets on my chin and bare cleavage for him to wipe away. He skips the napkin and licks his fingers after," Rosanna says as she stares at Hampton.

"When she drinks the champagne I pour for her, she tilts her head back," Hampton says. "It's so sexy because it makes her throat look so open and vulnerable, and then she just lets the liquid pour between her parted lips. She takes it down with no hesitation."

"OK. I think we need to stick to the rules and pass the basket, y'all," Chloe chimes in.

"I think it's sweet. After all these years they are still at each other like that," I say. There is a passion in their love for one another that turns me on to both Rosanna and Hampton. Everywhere they are, sexual tension seems to appear and linger a while.

"Well, if anybody has something nice to say about me, I want to know, straight up," Sam says.

"I second that motion," I say as I get up off the floor and

decide to start cleaning up to keep myself distracted from my sudden desire to devour the whole of the dessert table. It is covered in delectable selections of homemade sweet-mango tarts and peach cobbler that I'm certain will send me into the throes of an all-night sugar binge. I can never get enough of a good thing.

The party has moved out on the back deck, and I am in the kitchen by myself when he comes in. The whole time he is in there I can feel his eyes scanning the back of my body. Then he starts chatting about how good I'm looking.

"She is standing in the kitchen at the end of the party. She is just washing dishes, but she might as well be grinding against the cabinets in nothing but her ankle bracelets. Every time she shifts her weight from one leg to the other her fat ass jiggles under the thin fabric of her skirt and sends the blood rushing to my dick," Hampton says.

"Boy, you better quit it," I say. "Don't start nothing you can't finish."

I can't believe it when he comes over to the sink and starts touching my hair. I mean, shit, the only thing between us and the rest of the party, besides our marriages, is a sliding glass door. I am torn between feelings of shock and the tingles of anticipation spreading over my body like ripples in a lake, slow and steady, one after another. Then he grabs a handful of hair at the nape of my neck. I try to move, but I am in a trance. It is as if he is effortlessly taking me to the edge regardless of the consequences.

When Sam walks into the kitchen, I think Hampton will let go, but he just keeps his hold on me and asks Sam, "Man, doesn't she have some pretty-ass hair?"

Sam walks right over and grabs a handful for himself. "Pretty ass. Pretty hair. Pretty everything."

Sam is mature and reliable, and I admire that in him. He reminds me so much of my Rodney in that way. I really expect him to bring the whole situation back to home base, but he is open in a way I hadn't noticed before this moment. Suddenly he seems intensely sexual and mischievous. I blame it on the champagne. It makes everybody so lusciously edible and suckable to me, so I'm thinking it probably has him a little twisted, too.

"Uh…fellas. What's going on?"

"If you have to ask," Sam says.

"Well, I mean, did I miss a meeting?" I ask.

"We took a vote," Hampton says.

"Yes, and we decided it was time to take the game to another level," Sam says.

"I see. And when was somebody going to ask me if I was down with this?"

"You saying you're not?" Hampton asks.

I laugh a little and turn to look at Hampton. He is so lovely. His eyes are so certain. I can't understand how we have come to this, but I am open to the experience. I only worry that our marriages and our friendships will suffer if we take the game too far.

"Who came up with the game?" I ask. "Chloe?"

"Actually, it was Rosanna's idea," Hampton answers.

"Rosanna, huh?" I say. "What's the object of the game?"

"To see who the best lover is without fucking," Hampton says.

"Oh? I like the sound of that," I say. "What's considered fucking?"

"If you have to ask," Sam says again, and we all laugh.

I look out on the deck to see if we have become the cause for a pause, but to my surprise my husband is standing on the deck between Chloe and Rosanna, holding each around her waist and taking turns giving and receiving what looks like very sensuous kisses. For a moment, I am filled with instant fury because I know how delicious his kisses can be, but I let it go. I have my back to two irresistibly unavailable men, and they have me by the hair, standing against a kitchen sink full of sudsy water and slippery champagne flutes. All I can think of is floating in the ocean under the stars, surrendering myself to the rhythm of her waves and tasting the salty sweetness of her waters as she rocks me backward and forward into ecstasy.

Hampton takes his free hand and lifts my skirt over my ass and suggests we take things out on the deck to join the rest of the party. I push his hand away and smooth my skirt back down. The three of us file out the door. Once we are out there I lean back against the wooden rail. Rosanna comes closer and says, "It's about time we got this party started. I didn't think we were ever going to cross this godforsaken sexual divide."

Sam starts toward me, maybe for a kiss. I can't tell.

"Slow your roll, Sam. Damn," Rosanna says. "You're too tied up in all those layers." She is looking at me.

"I'm not taking my clothes off, Rosanna. This shit has gotten wild as hell."

"And why not?"

"Everybody else on this deck is fully clothed. Y'all are not gonna have me out here buck naked to be eaten alive by mosquitoes."

"Somebody get the citronella torches going," Rosanna says.

Etta James is singing "Don't Explain." We are face to face in the flattering light of floating candles, stars, and a misty moon. Rosanna is seducing me with her ability to make things happen, with her knack of getting people to do things—her way. Rodney, Sam, and Hampton are lighting torches when Rosanna asks me to take off my blouse.

"Rosanna—really now!"

"Just take it off. You can keep your bra on. It's just like a bikini top."

"I'll still be the only one taking anything off."

"Chloe, take off your shirt," Rosanna says.

"OK, but you know me: Once the bra is off, the party is on," Chloe says.

"That's the idea," Rosanna says.

"Well, if I had tits like yours, Chloe, I wouldn't need much convincing my damn self," I say.

"Tits aren't the only thing a woman has under her shirt, Meena," Rosanna says.

She had a point. Was she going to pull her own shirt off tonight? Had she come to terms with the loss of her own breasts to that extent? On film is one thing. In person is another. Thinking of our circumstances in comparison made me feel vain and silly. I was worried about nipples that didn't exactly point to the clouds anymore, and she was as flat as the day she was born and had no nipples at all.

"Why is it that every time I'm anywhere near you, I end up naked, one way or another?" I ask.

"Because you're so fucking beautiful and you don't know it," Rosanna says. "I would leave you alone if you would see yourself as you truly are. My work here would be done."

"Fucking drama queen. Rosanna's mission—to make all of her friends feel beautiful," I say.

"Well," she replies, "it ain't bad work if you can get it."

"Just the shirt, Rosanna. I'm not playing," I say as I begin to unbutton.

"Good girl," she says.

"Yeah, good girl," Hampton says. "I've learned to just do as I'm told. I don't know why you try so hard to resist."

When my shirt is off, I feel silly but daring. My husband, Rosanna, Hampton, Chloe, and Sam are forming a semicircle around the place where I am standing against the banister. Chloe has loosed her floating breasts. We have all seen those things so many times, they are almost an uneventful unveiling, but still quite amazing.

"Now you," I say to Rosanna.

"Me?"

"Unless you don't want to," I say, giving her some room to choose.

"I don't care. I just don't want anyone to get freaked out, and shit," Rosanna says.

"I can't speak for anybody else, but I think you're right when you say there's more under a woman's shirt than just tits," I say.

"Meena, you got me on that one," Rosanna says and lifts her yellow, sleeveless sweater over her head, revealing a completely flat chest and an equally flat and amazingly sculpted six-pack.

We are in our circle, a circle of friends and lovers, husbands and wives, three bare-chested women. In the light of the fire, stars, and moon, the scars where once there were breasts are like faded magnolias. There is nothing traumatic about the map of her journey. In reality, what her struggle with cancer has left behind is a kind of proof of courage. True beauty. The shots in the exhibit had seemed stark, barren. Here, in the flesh, there was warmth and abundant life.

"Well, damn," I say. "You weren't lying when you said you had been working out."

"Word," Hampton says. "She gets up at the crack of dawn every day and hits the road for a five-mile run and then hits the floor for at least a half hour of crunches."

"Well, what about you, Hampton?" Chloe asks.

"What *about* me?" he replies.

"Don't the fellas have anything to show?"

"What you looking for?" Sam asks.

"They want to see some strong backs and big arms," Rodney answers.

"You got that right," I say, "and plenty more, so take it off."

When everyone has taken off at least one article of clothing, we are standing still, just staring at one another. "What now?" I ask.

"Well, that depends," Rosanna says. "Do you want to give or receive first?"

"Shit. I think we all know the answer to that one," I say.

Rodney approaches me, and Rosanna quickly pulls him back to his place in the circle.

"Not you," Rosanna says. "You're her husband. You'd know exactly what to do to make her come right away. It has to be someone else."

Sam and Hampton both approach, and I am nervous. I don't want to appear uptight or inexperienced. I want to relax and just enjoy whatever is about to happen. Sam turns me around to face the railing, pulls my panties to the side, and smacks my fleshy behind a little to make it shake just before he puts two fingers between my thighs. Try as I might to hold onto my composure, my thighs are trembling. I am already slippery wet.

Then Hampton squats down, opens my legs, and licks my panties with his stiff tongue. When he finds my clitoris, he flicks at it until I squirm. Sam takes my chin and turns my head so that he can kiss me. He parts my lips with his tongue, and Hampton removes my panties, moves back in to devour me from the back, and we are caught up in the undercurrent of the slowest, deepest three-way kiss I could ever have imagined.

Then Rosanna grabs Rodney's crotch and undoes his pants. Within seconds she is sucking his already bulging penis. When I check on Rodney again, he and Chloe are fully engaged in a 69. I'm a little jealous, but I don't want to seem like a hypocrite, so instead of protesting, I suggest that our threesome move closer to join the twosome.

When Rodney turns his face from Chloe's bush long enough to notice our arrival, I am relieved to see that he has a smile on his wet face that tells me he's been doing just fine, but he's happy to see me.

I take one of Chloe's nipples between my index finger and thumb and begin to roll it back and forth with a little pressure.

"What happened to Rosanna?" I ask.

"Here I am," Rosanna answers. She is coming back on deck with her camera.

"Oh, hell no," I say. "Not the camera."

"Relax," Rosanna says and puts the camera on the side table near the door. "We're all friends here. I won't take any pictures below the neck. I promise. Plus, I'm not ready to start shooting yet, anyway."

"What the fuck," Chloe says. "I want to see my whole body." She laughs and gets us all relaxed again.

"Well, not me," I say. "I hope you don't think you're putting this shit up in some gallery."

"I don't care either way," Hampton says. "I think that would be funky. Pornographic maybe, but funky as hell."

"Me too," Rodney says.

"Oh, yeah?" I ask.

"Word. I don't have anything to hide," he answers.

"Oh, word? Let's see if you still talking shit opening night," I say. "Well, I guess it's just me and Sam from the neck up."

"That's all good for you, Meena," Sam says, "but Rosanna can take whatever shots she wants. I wanna see this freaky shit on film. Shit, somebody get the video camera. I want to take a few copies of the photos to work."

"You *would* want that shit, Sam," Rosanna says. "But I'm taking face shots only, and it's only for our private viewing, so everybody just get back to work."

Rosanna takes Chloe's other nipple, and we twist and pull at her firm breasts and watch them snap back with a bounce. We delight in the silky, salty softness of our bodies.

"I sure do miss my breasts," Rosanna says.

"I miss mine, too," I say. We sigh and move on.

"Y'all can have mine anytime you want them," Chloe says.

Hampton starts rubbing my clit from the back while he massages his penis, and Sam follows his lead and gets in position behind Rosanna. When we switch up, I take Hampton's long, brown, throbbing penis into my mouth and begin to suck deeply.

Rosanna gets to work on me with her wild tongue while I work on her husband, and I am thrilled to be sandwiched between two of the sexiest people I know. Rodney and Sam double-team Chloe, and she looks like she is in heaven.

Before long, Rosanna is teaching Chloe and me some new tricks as she focuses in on our faces with her digital camera. We are riding shins and grinding sidesplits. The boys are like misguided, frustrated missiles by now. I feel hands and tongues and fingers all over my body, and I am touching, rubbing, tweaking, sucking, grinding, licking, and kissing all at once. It is an exquisite overload of all my sexual senses.

One orgasm after another, we are climaxing, coming, getting our shit off, exploding, imploding, trembling, moaning, groaning, sighing, and singing ourselves into exhaustion. One-by-one, we each start to trail off for a little space, a smoke, or a drink. I am spent. When all the sucking and licking and kissing and hand jobs are finished, Rosanna gets her tripod, attaches the camera, and sets the timer.

Everyone is buttoning buttons and tucking in shirts and pulling down hiked skirts. Then I close my eyes and say to the group, "He's sexier than I ever imagined."

Then Hampton closes his eyes and says, "Every sound she utters, every gesture she makes embodies a sexual and spiritual revolution."

"My sentiments exactly," Rosanna says. "Now get into a group."

We get in a group, and Rosanna runs over to get in the picture.

After the photo is taken, Rosanna suggests we go in and see what she's got on disc. We all gather around the computer screen, and she pops in the disc. Rosanna had kept her promise. Our faces, one by one, appear, spreading themselves across the screen, unrecognizably distorted into otherworldly beings of pure expression like the faces of infants. We have become physically manifested emotions ranging from intense fury and agonizing sadness to drunken elation and soulful satisfaction. We watch in silence.

Rosanna pulls up the group shot and points out how we have all transformed back into our everyday personas, masks and roles intact. She says she's happy to have been allowed the honor and pleasure of seeing yet another side of her closest friends.

"Eros," she says, "is the power of complete and momentary surrender to the arms of the universe, a transcendental experience where our bodies and souls escape the confines of our constructed personalities."

"Hold on to your hats, ladies and gentlemen, we are orbiting out into Rosanna space!" Chloe says.

"I'm serious, Chloe. That's why Eros lives in so many forms," Rosanna says. "She lures us through all of our senses, even in our dreams. She's giving us as many opportunities as possible to be free and fully present in the truth of the moment."

"The truth isn't always beautiful," I say.

"Right," Rosanna continues, "but, Meena, whatever you see in your expression is momentary, fleeting, all-powerful because that's all there is. That's what makes it beautiful. The truth is beauty at its enlightening, disturbing, mind-blowing, heartbreaking best."

A week later, we get a thank-you note in the mail with

copies of the photographs. The note reads, "Thank you for celebrating *your beauty* with us. I think the photos would make a great exhibit. I'd like to call it 'Meeting Eros.' Think about it. Truthfully, Rosanna."

I want to put them away someplace where I will never look for them, but I cannot bring myself to so willingly and consciously hide such a powerful gift. That's Rosanna! She puts it right out there in plain sight. Sometimes beauty is hard to see head on—sort of like the sun, but no matter how many times we have been turned away by the painful glare, we find ourselves trying, again and again, to see what's there in the light. Maybe, like the sun, true beauty is too powerful to behold with the naked eye. Maybe to recognize and appreciate true beauty we need to feel it like warmth on our skin or taste it like ripened summer fruit or hear it in the songs of welcoming birds, or witness it in a different state of mind.

Maybe making love is a prelude to more than a physical climax; maybe it is a kind of birthing where I find myself crying into the miracle of being me. I take the photograph of my orgasmic face, which no matter how I look at it appears tortured and seems to be crying instead of climaxing, but then I think about how it feels to be so fully accessed, so lovingly tasted, so deeply felt, and so willingly heard, and the beauty is revealed in the feelings remembered.

About the Authors

OPAL PALMER ADISA was born in Kingston, Jamaica. She is the cofounder of Watoto Wa Kuumba, a children's theater group that she directed from 1979 to 1982. She is the author of *Pina, the Many-eyed Fruit* (1985), *Bake-Face and Other Guava Stories* (1986), *Traveling Women* (1989), *Tamarind and Mango Women* (1992), *It Begins with Tears* (1997), and *Leaf-of-Life* (2000). Her poetry, stories, and articles have been anthologized widely.

TA'SHIA ASANTI is the recipient of the Audre Lorde Black Quill Award, the Seed Scholarship award, and an award for best erotic fiction from the Literary Exchange. In 2002, she was nominated for the Courage in Journalism award. Asanti has written one novel, a collection of short stories, a book of poetry, and a book of creative nonfiction titled *The Book of the Sacred Door*. She lives in Denver with her partner and daughter.

CAMILLE BANKS-LEE is a writer, teacher, and cofounder of Daughters of the Nile, Inc., an academic and creative arts mentoring organization for adolescent girls in Mount Vernon, New York. She and her husband, Malcolm, live in New York with their son, Langston.

JAMYLA BENNU is a New York–based writer, dancer, and Web/print designer.

TARA BETTS, a Cave Canem fellow, is a writer and teacher in Chicago. Her work has appeared in *These Hands I Know, Obsidian III, Columbia Poetry Review, That Takes Ovaries!, Role Call, Bum Rush the Page, Power Lines, Poetry Slam,* and Steppenwolf Theatre's *Words on Fire.* She cohosts an all-women's open mic/performance space called Women OutLoud, and represented Chicago at the 1999 and 2000 National Poetry Slams.

JANEÉ BOLDEN is a graduate of the Creative Writing Program at New York University. She was most recently published in *Role Call: A Generational Anthology of Social and Political Black Literature and Art.* She lives in New York City.

D. H. BRENT has written for a national trade association newspaper and owns and manages a graphic design/marketing firm. She has composed numerous poems, and recently began writing erotic short stories. She lives in Laurel, Maryland, and is working on her first novel.

C. C. CARTER has retired from the slam competition scene, but not before winning the Fifth Annual Guild Complex Gwendolyn Brooks Open Mic Competition and Lambda Book Report's First Annual National Slam Competition at the Behind Our Mask conference, as well as several local and national slams. She is an adjunct professor at Columbia College in Chicago, where she teaches performance poetry workshops. She is a program director for adult literacy.

R. ERICA DOYLE is a writer of Trinidadian descent who resides in New York City. She teaches writing to teens and adults, is a fellow of Cave Canem, and has received awards from the Astraea and Hurston/Wright foundations. Her work appears in various publications, including *Best American Poetry 2001, Gumbo: A Celebration of African American Writing, Bum Rush the Page, Role Call, Ploughshares, Callaloo* and *Ms. Magazine.* She is currently at work on a novel.

MICHELE ELLIOTT is a writer, teacher, and visual artist. She teaches creative writing for several local arts organizations and is a grant writer for a community arts center in Washington, D.C. She is working on a book-length manuscript of poetry. She earned an M.F.A. in Creative Writing from the University of Pittsburgh.

DOROTHY RANDALL GRAY is a motivational speaker and the author of six books of poetry, fiction, and nonfiction, including the best-selling *Soul Between the Lines: Freeing Your Creative Spirit Through Writing.* Her work has been published in numerous anthologies and periodicals, including *SisterFire, Drum Voices, Personal Journaling, Conditions, HealthQuest,* and the *New York Times.* Gray facilitates writing workshops, empowerment seminars, and healing rituals throughout the United States and abroad. She is founder of the Heartland Institute for Transformation, a spiritual center for the promotion of creativity, empowerment, and healing through the written word.

CAROL SMITH PASSARIELLO, editor of *Sister Soul Journeys,* teaches in the English Department at State University of New York, Westchester. Her work has appeared in *Honey* and *Black Issues Book Review* as well as in the film *The Best Man.*

TRACY PRICE-THOMPSON is the author of the recent Random House release *Black Coffee.* She is currently coediting *Proverbs for the People: An Anthology of Contemporary African-American Fiction.* Her work has been recently published in *Children of the Dream: Our Stories of Growing Up Black in America* and *Fortitude.* She received an M.S.W. from Rutgers University and is a Ralph Bunche Fellow as well as a Hurston/Wright Awardee.

SHAWN E. RHEA is a journalist, essayist, poet, and fiction writer. Her work has been featured in *Anansi: Fiction of the African Diaspora, The Source, Essence, Black Enterprise, Teen People, BET.com,* and the *New Orleans Times Picayune.* A graduate of Howard University and Columbia University's Graduate School of Journalism, she is currently completing the Thurgood Marshall Scholarship Fund's forthcoming book *I'll Find a Way or Make One: A History of Historically Black Colleges and Universities.* A Detroit native, Rhea lives and writes variously in New York City and Detroit.

KIINI IBURA SALAAM is a writer, painter, and traveler from New Orleans. Her fiction has been anthologized in *Black Silk, When Butterflies Kiss, Dark Matter,* and *Dark Eros.* Her essays have been published in *Role Call, Men We Cherish, Utne Reader, Essence,* and *Ms.* She is currently crafting her first novel, *Bloodlines,* a collection of erotic short stories. She is the author of the KIS.list, a weekly e-report on life as a writer. Her work can be accessed at www.kiiniibura.com. She lives in Brooklyn.

DONNA SHERARD holds an M.P.H. degree in reproductive health, with a particular interest in HIV prevention and education for women of color. She lives in Kampala, Uganda, writing and working in reproductive health programming and policy for women in East Africa.

FOLADE MONDISA SPEAKS-LOVE, a poet and painter, received an M.F.A. degree from the School of the Art Institute of Chicago. A Cave Canem fellow, she has published in such visual art and literary journals as *Nexus: Literary and Art Journal* and *Bum Rush the Page: A Def Poetry Jam,* as well as on a CD of poetry and sound about Jean-Michel Basquiat. She is cofounder of the Chicago-based multimedia artist collective *ink and image productions.*

KIMBERLEY WHITE is the author of the sensuous romance novel *Sweet Tomorrows.* As the founder of Kimberley's Critiquing and Consulting, she teaches writing courses and acts as a conference planner. She lives in Detroit.

ROBIN G. WHITE is the author of *Resurrection: A Collection of Work,* a finalist for the 2002 Georgia Author of the Year Award. Her stories have been widely anthologized, and she has written for the *Gay Community News, Dorchester Community News,* and *City Life/Vida Urbana.* Her plays have been produced in Atlanta, New York, and Boston. She is a vocalist for the spoken-word band Sweet Black Molasses, and has performed with Adodi Muse, Ten Percent Revue, playwright Dr. Shirlene Holmes, and the Zuna Institute. She lives in Atlanta, where she is co-owner of Kings Crossing Publishing.

About the Editor

SAMIYA A. BASHIR, coeditor of *Role Call: A Generational Anthology of Social and Political Black Literature and Art*, with Tony Medina and Quraysh Ali Lansana, is a poet, writer, and editor (known for her work at *Black Issues Book Review, Ms.,* and *Curve* magazines). She is completing her debut collection of poetry. A Cave Canem fellow, she has won numerous awards for her poetry, including being honored as Poet Laureate of the University of California and winning the 2002 Astraea Poetry Award. Her poetry, articles, essays and stories. have been published in many anthologies, magazines, and journals, including *Obsidian III, Kuumba #4, ColorLines, Contemporary American Women Poets, Bum Rush the Page: A Def Poetry Jam, Arise, Other Countries: Voices Rising, Best Lesbian Erotica 2003, Poetry for the People: A Revolutionary Blueprint, Lambda Book Report, The American Journal of Public Health,* and *San Francisco Bay Guardian.*